**Praise for *New York Times* bestselling author
Leslie Kelly**

"Sexy, funny and a little outrageous,
Leslie Kelly is a must read!"
—*New York Times* bestselling author Carly Phillips

"Leslie Kelly is a rising star of romance!"
—#1 *New York Times* bestselling author
Debbie Macomber

"A sexy read with an alpha male,
realistic characters and an entertaining plot."
—*Harlequin Junkie* on *Double Take*

"Kelly succeeds with this sexy story,
keeping the tension high."
—*RT Book Reviews* on *Waking Up to You*

"Kelly employs a great deal of heart and humor
to achieve balance with this incendiary romance.
Great characters, many of whom fans will
recognize, and a vibrant narrative kept
this reader glued to each and every word."
—*The Romance Reader's Connection*
on *Overexposed*

D0124156

Blaze®

Dear Reader,

Over my many years writing books for Harlequin, I have really enjoyed creating holiday-themed stories, with several Christmas novels, and some revolving around Halloween.

This year, knowing I had a November release, I decided to try something a little different. Falling right between Halloween and Christmas is one of my favorite holidays: Thanksgiving. I'd never done a Thanksgiving book, nor could I envision a whole Turkey Day–themed novel. But the idea of capturing the entire holiday season, from the end of October through Christmas, excited me. I relished the chance to take one couple from the dizzying excitement of a naughty costumed encounter at a Halloween party through to the happy excitement of Thanksgiving and right into the tender loveliness of Christmas.

I truly love how this turned out, and so enjoyed bringing Lulu and Chaz through my three favorite holidays of the year. I hope their story makes your holiday season a little more sweet-and-spicy, too.

Best wishes,

Leslie Kelly

Leslie Kelly

—

Oh, Naughty Night!

HARLEQUIN® BLAZE™

Recycling programs
for this product may
not exist in your area.

ISBN-13: 978-0-373-79824-7

Oh, Naughty Night!

Copyright © 2014 by Leslie A. Kelly

Printed in U.S.A.

ABOUT THE AUTHOR

New York Times bestselling author Leslie Kelly has written dozens of books and novellas for the Harlequin Blaze, Temptation and HQN lines. Known for her sparkling dialogue, fun characters and steamy sensuality, she has been honored with numerous awards, including a National Readers' Choice Award, a Colorado Award of Excellence, a Golden Quill and an *RT Book Reviews* Career Achievement Award in Series Romance. Leslie has also been nominated four times for the highest award in romance fiction, the RWA RITA® Award. Leslie lives in Maryland with her own romantic hero, Bruce, and their daughters.

Visit her online at www.lesliekelly.com or at her blog, www.plotmonkeys.com.

Books by Leslie Kelly

HARLEQUIN BLAZE

To get the inside scoop on Harlequin Blaze and its talented writers, be sure to check out blazeauthors.com.

To the younger members of my big extended family...

Elliott, Kyleigh, Trey, Addison, Isiah, Christopher, Jordyn, D4 and Baby Lundh...

I hope the holiday memories you're building with your wonderful parents are as magical as mine always were. Aunt Loulou loves you all!

1

"THERE'S NOTHING WORSE than having the hots for a sexy guy, and then finding out he has the personality of a turnip."

Lucille Vandenberg—known to her friends and family as Lulu, which wasn't great, but was certainly better than Lucille—didn't try to keep the disappointment out of her voice as she griped to her friends, Viv and Amelia. Honestly, a guy who looked as good as the man holding the guitar at the crowded bar should have boatloads of brains and charm to go with his amazing body. But this one? Ugh. She'd had more scintillating conversations with her houseplants.

"Sorry he turned out to be a disappointment," said Amelia, her pretty, gentle face full of commiseration and support.

Viv wasn't as comforting. "If the turnip's hung like a porn star, you can handle a root vegetable, Lulu. I mean, it's not as if you want a life partner here."

Lulu wasn't convinced, mainly because, once again, she'd set herself up for disappointment. For the past month, since she'd moved to Washington, D.C., she'd been on the lookout for an interesting guy to help break her long romantic dry streak. For what seemed like forever, she had been so focused on getting through grad school, and then on her internship in Rwanda, and then on her new job with a local NGO. She hadn't allowed herself a single date in ages. Of course, that also could have been because her last serious relationship had been with someone who'd been so self-absorbed and career-focused, he hadn't even known her middle name, her favorite color, or much of anything else about her a year after they'd been together.

But now she needed sex. Badly. Needed to have it with somebody who would make her forget she hadn't had it for so long…or at least make her believe the wait had really been worthwhile. She could deal with him not caring about her middle name or favorite colors, at least for one night.

"I just wanted to meet somebody nice, sexy and smart, and have a welcome-to-Washington adventure," she mused.

And when she'd come into this Dupont Circle bar earlier in the week and met the super-hot guitar player, she'd thought she might have found the perfect person with whom to do it.

But when they'd talked tonight, he'd turned out to be as adventurous as a trip to the dentist. Not even a trip for a filling, or a root canal, just a plain old check-up. Yawn. The monosyllabic conversation they'd shared when she arrived tonight had crushed her fantasies completely.

"Who cares about his IQ?" Viv added. "It's his looks and *size* that matter."

"Maybe to *you*," said Amelia, her tone a bit disapproving.

Really, the two former college roommates couldn't be more dissimilar, and Lulu wondered how they'd survived. They were like Oscar and Felix, only female. One was sexually conservative while the other was a bit of a slut. A definite odd couple.

"I wish I could be as brutally shallow as you, Viv," Lulu said. "But I need conversation to go with the pecs and schlong."

Viv grinned, impossible to insult. She *was* the queen of mean. "Fine, forget him. But don't give up. The night is young."

Maybe. But she didn't want merely smarts, she also wanted a guy who was honest and direct, who didn't play games with his intentions. Someone who knew what he wanted and went after it…not a wishy-washy dude who couldn't even speak unless the subject was his favorite band.

Why the hell was it so hard to find somebody like that?

Amelia raised her voice to be heard over the crowd, which was growing louder with every costumed body that crammed into the trendy bar. "There will be lots of guys here tonight. You'll find somebody better."

"I doubt it."

"Have another drink. They'll *all* start to look better after three of those things," said Viv, gesturing toward Lulu's glass.

Lulu was already feeling the effects of two. Unfortunately, they were making her more choosy, not less. "I'm not the one-night-stand-with-a-stranger type."

Viv raised a brow and gestured toward the guitarist.

"He wasn't a stranger," Lulu insisted. "I sorta knew him."

"You exchanged five words with him before tonight," Viv said with a smirk.

"But I knew his name."

"Only his last one."

"Yeah, what's up with that?"

Viv shrugged. "Schaefer's all mysterious about his first name. I bet it's something stupid like Fred or Homer or Ralph."

Amelia, smiling sweetly, said, "Maybe he's just trying to keep some things private, since he's in the spotlight."

Perhaps. But she suspected the broodiness and first-name mystery were intended to heighten interest in an otherwise pretty uninteresting guy. It had certainly worked on her, at least until she'd heard him say more than "Got a request?"

Sighing, she swirled her Devil's Brew—the drink on special for tonight's big Halloween bash—and sipped it. She was careful not to splash any of the red liquid onto the half-mask that covered her face from mid-forehead down to the tip of her nose. Lulu had gone to a lot of trouble with this costume, having fully intended to look as sexy and wicked as she could in hopes of stirring some naughty thoughts in the guitarist. She was a witch, but her green mask wasn't the least bit scary—no long nose or warts. She'd gone instead for a Mardi Gras type facial covering, with sequins and cat-shaped eye openings. Beneath her pointy hat, her hair was curled and teased, wild and untamed. She'd also sprayed a coating of glittery red hairspray onto it, making herself even more unrecognizable.

Schaefer had noticed. She'd seen appreciation and heat in his eyes. His brain might be all vegetable, but his body apparently had some blood flowing through its roots. Er, veins.

That probably would have been enough for most sex-starved twenty-six-year-old women. Maybe it would have been enough for grad-school Lulu. But she'd changed since she'd returned from her internship in Rwanda. Working in a country filled with people who had so little, and then for a nonprofit group that gave microloans to similar, desperately-hopeful populations, would do that to a person.

She supposed she really had grown up. But that didn't mean she didn't still have the desire to go out and cut loose, if only to escape the sadness and deprivation she often witnessed in her job. But not with a turnip.

"Whoa, striptease at eleven o'clock," Viv said, her dark eyes widening.

"Wow, I thought this place was more upscale than that. Maybe we should go someplace else before then," said Amelia, sounding a little shocked.

"I wasn't talking about the time, Miss Literal." Viv pointed. "I mean at *my* eleven o'clock."

Lulu and Amelia both turned, peering through the crowd, trying to see what had caught Viv's attention. At first, Lulu merely spied a sea of devils, vampires, sexy nurses and construction workers. Then she spotted a figure standing alone near the dance floor, facing away from her. And she simply couldn't look away.

The guy had donned a white sheet for the event, going for the age-old ghost outfit that had gone out of style before Lulu was in elementary school. But even a single sheet was apparently too much. As if he'd felt he'd done his holiday duty by appearing in a requisite costume for a little while, he'd begun to pull the sheet up to remove it. He'd already revealed long legs covered in soft, loose-fitting jeans that draped across powerful, muscular thighs. Not to mention an utterly delish male ass lovingly cupped by that faded denim.

As he stretched his arms up, he caught the bottom hem of his shirt, which was now rising with the sheet—perhaps by design, but more likely by accident. Whatever the reason, she, Viv, Amelia and, she noted, every woman around them, watched him with avid attention as he bared smooth, supple skin, golden and slick with sweat from the hot, crowded bar. His jeans hung low on lean hips; his waist was slim, every inch of him hard.

Lulu reached blindly for her drink, sipping, but she

didn't take her eyes off the ghost. The sheet and shirt went higher—*oh, God, that back.* It rippled with muscle, every bit of him powerful and sexy. In that body, strength wasn't just implied, it was promised, and though she wasn't a petite woman, she suddenly felt very feminine and fragile in comparison.

Catching a glimpse of ink on the back of his shoulder, she waited for more of it to be revealed. She held her breath, dying to see the broad shoulders and bare, flexing arms.

Unfortunately, he appeared to realize he'd been putting on a show. The man yanked the shirt back into place with one hand, and whipped the sheet the rest of the way off with the other. She almost heard a universal sigh of disappointment from every double-Y chromosome in the joint.

"A blond," Amelia said with a pleased little sigh.

"I like blonds," Viv purred.

Lulu never had before, but she was definitely seeing the appeal. "I'm quickly developing an appreciation for them."

Viv tried to stake her claim. "If he has a face to go with the rest of the package, I'll be poisoning your drinks so I can get to him first."

Lulu waited, sending mental signals for the guy to turn around so she could judge if the front was as amazing as the back. He didn't accommodate her fully, but he did glance toward the guitarist, nodding hello to Schaefer. Lulu got just a brief glimpse of his profile, but it was enough to make her gasp in shock.

Lurching from her chair, she said, "It can't be."

"Can't be who?" asked Amelia.

"Chaz."

Viv frowned. "A guy who looks like that is named Jazz?"

"Chaz," Lulu insisted, shaking the confusion out of her

head and slowly lowering herself back down as her two friends eyed her curiously. "No, I'm wrong. I have to be. No way is that Chaz Browning."

"Hmm," Amelia mused, "that name sounds familiar."

"He's a journalist—some of his stuff has been in *Time* magazine and now I think he works for the Associated Press, or maybe Reuters," Lulu said, still trying to get the crazy thought that the Chaz she'd known as a kid could possibly have grown up to be the stud she'd just been ogling.

"Who are we talking about, the guy over there?" asked Viv.

"No, it's just a resemblance." She sipped again, willing her heart to stop thudding. "Chaz Browning was a boy from my hometown in western Maryland, literally the boy next door. Our parents are best friends, but we always tormented each other."

Well, mostly she'd tormented him. She smiled, thinking how silly she'd been to equate Chaz Browning with the red-hot dude across the bar.

"I've barely seen him since he graduated from high school nine years ago. But our families are still close. My mother told his mother that I was moving here, and he emailed me with info about his Realtor. That's how I got my apartment."

"And Chaz is definitely not Mr. Sexy Ghost?" Viv said, still focused on the handsome stranger, now ringed by a trio of costumed women. Lulu frowned, seeing the way they leaned against him, brushing body parts against his thick arms and strong legs.

None of your business, she reminded herself, turning in her chair to face her friend, and not the walking sexsicle.

"No way. Chaz was a total nerd. Skinny, awkward."

He definitely didn't have tons of muscles or an ass that

could make a wolf-whistler of a nun. Sweet, quiet Chaz had as much in common with ghost-guy as Brad Pitt did with Elmer Fudd.

"Well, Mr. Ghost is definitely not a wimp," Viv said.

Chaz hadn't been a wimp, either, exactly. Memories flashed through her mind and she felt the same pang of guilt she always felt when she remembered the boy she'd known. She'd harassed him mercilessly—like the time Chaz had gone up onto the roof of the garage to retrieve a football. She'd waited until he was up there, and had then taken the ladder away. Chaz, not wanting to admit defeat to a mere girl, had jumped, landing hard enough on the ground that he fell and cracked his tailbone.

Her mom had accused Lulu of picking on Chaz only because she had a crush on him. She'd denied it, though she'd always thought he *was* kind of cute when he blushed. Which was often.

Suddenly, Viv's eyes went even rounder, and her mouth fell open. "Oh, my God, the front half is even better than the rear."

Lulu spun around on her seat again, wanting a better look. The hot stranger had turned toward them. She saw his face, noted the features—the green eyes with laugh lines beside them, the dimple in one cheek, the small cleft in his chin.

Confusion raced through her. The square, slightly grizzled jaw did not compute, nor did the wide, oh-so-kissable mouth, the flashing green eyes, the utter, rugged handsomeness of the man.

All unfamiliar…yet very familiar indeed.

"No way," she mumbled. "It just *can't* be."

She stared and stared. And gradually, the truth forced its way into her consciousness.

She might not recognize the body, but she knew that

face, that smile, that dimple. She could no longer deny that the sexy ghost was, indeed, Chaz, the boy-next-door. The one she'd tormented, the one who'd ignored her until she'd been as rotten as possible to get his attention, the one she'd hoped to meet again here in D.C. if only so she could make up for being such a little snot when they were kids. But she needed to work up to it and wasn't prepared to start tonight. Unfortunately the mask probably didn't hide enough of her face that he wouldn't recognize her.

It was like some kind of morality play or Aesop's fable. She'd been the mean girl to a rather forgettable boy, and Chaz Browning had grown up to be the hottest, most *un*forgettable man she'd ever laid eyes on.

"It's him. It's really him."

"Your old friend?" asked Amelia.

"Something like that." Friend wasn't the word she'd use.

"He's totally checking you out."

Lulu shook off her shock and paid attention again, realizing that Viv was right. Chaz was eyeing her, a smile tugging at the corners of that incredible mouth. So maybe he had a short memory and didn't recall that he had reason to hate her guts. Or maybe he'd just grown up and looked back at their childhood days through a softer lens, as she had.

She gave him a bright, sunny smile back, shoving away her sexual interest, forcing herself to remember this was an old frenemy. No way did she want him to know she'd been drooling over him.

He started to come over, probably to say hello, ask how she was settling in to city life, maybe make small talk about the old days. She glanced away, focusing on her drink, running her fingertips over the condensation on the glass, feigning a nonchalance she definitely did not feel.

"Hi," a man's voice said a moment later. It was Chaz's

voice, with many years' worth of maturity added on. He stood behind her, and she felt the warmth of his big, broad body.

Willing her cheeks not to pinken and her voice not to quiver, she glanced up at him. "Hi, yourself."

"Happy Halloween."

"Same to you."

He gestured toward her glass. "I'd offer to buy you a drink, but it seems you're full-up. How's the special?"

"Remember the taste of kids' cherry-flavored cough syrup?"

"Uh-huh."

"That tasted better."

"Think I'll stick to beer."

"Good choice," she said. "I like your costume."

He glanced down at his loose cotton T-shirt and those wickedly worn jeans. "Guy next door?"

Huh. Funny. "I meant the ghost. Why'd you take it off?"

"I'm not so great with scissors. I cut the eye holes too small and couldn't see where the hell I was going."

She laughed. Chaz had never had much hand-eye coordination. But she'd bet he could do some utterly amazing things with those hands now, and the heavily-lashed green eyes were enough to make a girl melt.

"Still a fan of the homemade costume, huh?"

"My mother would kill me if I got a store-bought one."

Yeah. She remembered. Their moms had coordinated outfits every holiday, though they couldn't always please everybody. One year, when she'd wanted to be Sailor Moon, she'd had to go as a stupid Power Ranger instead because it was Chaz's favorite show. She'd even had to be the yellow ranger, since his spoiled sister had called dibs on the pink one.

She'd repaid him by stealing every one of the chocolate bars from his trick-or-treat bag and replacing them with raisins.

Lord, she'd been such a little terror.

Chaz hadn't been the only one with a pesky younger sibling—her brother was his sister's age. The four of them had grown up together, squabbling, competing. It hadn't been all-out war, though, until their siblings started dating in high school—and then had a messy breakup. She wasn't sure Lawrence had ever got over Sarah dumping him. But that had happened after Chaz had left home. He might not even realize that his sister was a heartbreaking butthead.

"I had no time to figure out something more elaborate," he explained. "I only decided to come here about an hour ago."

"That's some serious last-minute costume design," she said.

"Hey, cut me some slack. I just got back into town this morning after a long overseas trip. I hadn't even remembered it was Halloween until I got home and saw the decorations. Good thing I had a clean sheet in my linen closet."

"And good thing it was plain white and didn't have Teenage Mutant Ninja Turtles all over it."

He barked a laugh, raising a brow, as if surprised she'd remembered those sheets or those turtles he'd been so obsessed with.

"I think I've outgrown my mutant turtle days."

"Strictly into human ninjas now, huh?"

His eyes twinkled. "Yeah, that's it. Unfortunately, I haven't found a California-king sheet set with little black-cloaked ninja dudes on them."

Mmm. Big bed. For a big guy. With big hands. *And a big...*

"I'm afraid I'm stuck with boring, non-decorative sheets."

She swallowed and forced her mind back to light small talk and away from thoughts of his sheets. Or his bed. Him in his bed… "I'll keep an eye out for ninjas for you. Unless you'd prefer Transformers."

"Nah, I'm good." He grinned and the earth rocked a bit. "Though, if you see black satin, let me know. I might be tempted to play ninja."

She gulped, wondering when on earth he'd gotten so damned confident. He was easygoing, sexy, masculine and totally comfortable in a room full of people. No longer the male wallflower, the kid whose shoelaces were tied together by bullies, or who got picked last for the baseball team because he'd dropped a fly ball and lost the big game in fourth grade.

No. He was all sexy, powerful, enticing, grown-up man. And she just had no idea what to think about that.

"You must be awfully tired," Viv said, interjecting herself into the playful conversation. "After traveling all day."

Funny, Lulu had almost forgotten she was there. Amelia, too. Chaz, while offering the other two women a polite smile, hadn't paid a moment of attention to either of them. That made Lulu feel better—her old childhood nemesis/friend hadn't come over merely to get Lulu to introduce him to Viv, who usually cast other females in the shade. Lulu wasn't sure whether it was because Viv was so beautiful, or because she was such a stone-cold bitch to most men that they felt challenged to break through the ice. Her costume, a sexy devil, seemed more than a little appropriate. As did Amelia's, who was dressed as a cute rag doll, complete with a yarn wig she'd made herself using supplies from her craft shop.

Hmm. She wondered if Chaz would say she, too, was appropriately costumed for her personality.

"I guess I am tired," he admitted.

"I'll say. Sounds like all you can think of is your bed," Viv said, her smile still knowing, a wicked gleam in her eyes.

Chaz didn't nibble at the bait. In fact, he didn't even seem to notice he was being flirted with. "I probably shoulda crashed, but I was in need of some American holiday fun. There's not a single piece of candy corn in Pakistan. So I decided to come out to combat the jet lag."

"And eat candy corn?" Lulu asked, unhappy Viv was working her vixen magic on her old friend. Well, her old *something.*

"Exactly. Have any on you?"

"I'm all out. I guess you'll have to trick-or-treat through the neighborhood on your way home."

"I forgot my sack."

"Then you're just out of luck."

He sighed. "Day late and a treat short. Story of my life."

Yeah. Because of mean girls who stole his candy bars.

She didn't bring that up, though. No point reminding him of her antics if there was any chance in hell he'd forgotten them.

As if. That'd be like Batman forgetting the Joker's antics. Once an arch nemesis, always an arch nemesis.

Not that she'd ever really considered Chaz her nemesis, arch or otherwise. But he might have one or two reasons to think *she* was. Including a crooked tailbone.

"Well, pull up a chair and join us," said Viv, scooting over to make room for him. She cast Lulu a piercing look, waiting for her to officially introduce them.

She was about to, but he cut her off.

"Actually, I just wanted to see if you'd like to dance," he said, staring down at Lulu, his gaze wavering between friendly and intense. She had to wonder if he, too, had been shocked by the changes nine years had wrought. She didn't much resemble the stringy-haired, braces-wearing seventeen-year-old he probably remembered from his high school graduation party. The one when she'd pushed him into the swimming pool, fully clothed, because he'd called her flat-chested.

To be fair, she *had* been a late bloomer. Of course, he hadn't really needed to point that out in front of all their friends and family.

She sat up a little straighter and thrust that no-longer-flat chest out the tiniest bit.

His gaze shifted. He noticed. She noticed him noticing.

"Well?" he asked, his voice dropping to a more intimate tone. "What do you say?"

"Uh…you really want to dance? With *me?*"

She was pretty sure the only time they'd ever danced together was when they'd had to be square-dancing partners in gym class in middle school. It hadn't gone well. Holding hands with Chaz had been way too weird for her twelve-year-old self. Her hands had gotten sweaty, her breath short, and she'd had the strangest fluttering in her stomach.

She now suspected what the sweating and fluttering had been all about. She *had* liked Chaz's blushes, despite what she'd said to her mother. But back then, never wanting to admit such a thing, she'd convinced herself that holding hands with Chaz Browning was enough to make her want to throw up.

So she'd done what any bratty twelve-year-old would do. She'd stuck out her foot and tripped him during their do-si-do.

Little bitch.

"You know how to dance, right?" Another green twinkle—how had she never noticed he had the most interesting golden streaks that cut through the irises, looking like starbursts? "I mean, it's pretty easy—you just try to find the beat in the music and move around to it."

She licked her lips, hearing the band finishing "Time Warp," which immediately made her think of pelvic thrusts—not something she should be thinking about when it came to Chaz. Luckily the musicians segued right into a torchy version of "Witchcraft." That somehow seemed appropriate, given her costume, and the fact that she felt as if someone had cast a spell on her. The song was slower, jazzier, and would necessitate close-up dancing, with hands and bodies in direct contact. And though her mind decided that was even riskier than pelvic thrusts, her legs launched her out of her chair immediately.

"Sure."

She let him take her hand and pull her toward the crowded dance floor. When he grabbed her hips and pulled her close, she swallowed hard, trying to maintain her smile. Could he feel her crazily-beating heart or see the way her pulse thrummed in her throat? And was there any way in hell he didn't know that some of her most female parts were standing at attention as their bodies brushed together?

Lulu waited for him to say something—*Welcome to D.C., How's the new place?, How are your folks?* But he remained silent, merely moving his thigh between her legs as they swayed.

Lord have mercy. Though she'd often imagined having Chaz's throat between her hands so she could strangle him for saying something that totally pissed her off, she'd never fantasized about having any part of him between her thighs.

He'd been gone from her life before she'd realized stomach flutters and thigh clenching were definite signs of lust.

But now her body was reacting to him in a way she'd never allowed her mind to. There was no mistaking her reaction for anything except excitement. Her palms were sweating and her whole body felt hot and sticky, as though if she didn't get her clothes off, she would melt right into a puddle of want in the middle of the dance floor.

God, he was so big and strong compared to the boy she'd known. Powerful, male, appealing enough to stop hearts. His chest was so broad it could be used as a life raft. She couldn't help twining her fingers in his longish hair, tousled from the sheet, shaggy from a few months' travel.

The truth slammed into her, hard and life-changing.

She wanted him. Badly. Lulu wanted to go to bed with Chaz Browning and see if all the years of angry tension between them could be erased by erotic tension.

If only he were some random guy she'd just met, and the baggage of an entire childhood of fighting and competing, not to mention family drama, didn't stand between them. If only he were just a sexy stranger like Schaefer, albeit one with charm, easy wit and personality.

Unfortunately, he wasn't a stranger. Despite how closely he held her, Chaz couldn't possibly have forgotten her childhood shenanigans and his own disdain toward her. There was no way he'd look at her as anything but the bane of his youth and the scorn of his adulthood. Plus there was the family-connection burden of looking after her. His email had said he'd promised his mom he'd do exactly that once he was back in the country, like she was some high schooler on a field trip to the big bad city. An inconvenience. A brat.

No, anything remotely resembling a sexual connection between her and Chaz was simply out of the question. She was just going to have to go home and get cozy with her vibrator, or say to hell with it and bang the boring guitar player. Anything to avoid letting Chaz realize he'd affected her so deeply. That would be worse than the sweaty hands/ square dancing incident.

"The music's good tonight," he finally said. "Schaefer and his band have improved since the last time I heard them play."

"You know him?"

"Yeah, he's sort of a regular in the neighborhood and he was a soloist for a while. But he was a bit of a hippie. He'd get into trouble, sneaking out of upbeat background music and into some depressing, sixties, psychedelic-mushroom ballad once in a while. Talk about a mood killer. The bar owners threatened to ban him."

"Do you know his first name?"

Chaz grinned. "I do."

"What is it?"

"If I told you, I'd have to kill you. He made me promise."

"Must be a doozy."

He nodded slowly. "Let's just say…it's appropriate."

"Can't I bribe it out of you?"

"What'll you give me?"

"All the Tootsie Rolls from my goodie bag?"

"I'm not interested in candy," he told her, that half smile lingering on a mouth so kissable it made her own go dry.

"I thought you were jonesing for candy corn."

"Maybe I'd rather taste something else sweet."

Whoa. The twinkle in his eye and the flash of that dimple took the light comment and brought it up to flirtatious—maybe even suggestive—level. It was totally unlike anything he'd *ever* said to her. She had to wonder how many drinks he'd had, or if he'd been drinking them on an empty, jet-lagged stomach. She just didn't believe a sober Chaz would've made that kind of comment—not to her, anyway.

"Like what?" she asked, her tone just as flirty and suggestive, calling his bluff. She knew he'd put a stop to the conversation any second, but couldn't deny she was having fun while it lasted.

"That drink left your lips looking very red and delicious."

Good God, was he going to kiss her? The way his gaze focused in on her face said he was considering it, and her heart pounded in her chest. It was crazy. They hadn't even played doctor as kids, much less snuck even the most innocent of kisses. But he was eyeing her mouth as if he was parched and needed to positively drink from her.

"I have to admit, this conversation is taking me by surprise," she said, hearing the breathiness in her own voice and wondering what he would make of it.

"You can't be surprised that I think you're beautiful."

"I most certainly am," she said with a forced smile. Chaz, the boy who'd once called her a soul-sucking leech, thought she was beautiful?

Yeah. He had to be drunk.

"Every man here thinks it," he said, sounding totally serious. "I saw you the minute I walked in and couldn't take my eyes off you." Glancing down at her body, he smiled wickedly. "You surprised me. I always assumed witches were old and ugly."

"Only bad witches are ugly," she pointed out, catching his *Wizard of Oz* reference.

"And you're a very good witch?"

"Some would debate that. Maybe I'm a little of both."

"Which witch are you tonight?"

"Which witch do you hope I am?"

His green eyes glittered under the dance floor lights. "Maybe a little of both."

Hmm.

"Just remind me not to drop a house on you."

"Or douse me with water," she said with a grin, liking how easy they were with each other. Old friends flirting a little, reminiscing a little. Because they *were* both exploring a shared memory.

It had been her eleventh Halloween. She'd wanted to be a Spice Girl, but in a repetition of the Sailor Moon fiasco, of course the boys wouldn't go for what she wanted, so they'd all done a *Wizard of Oz* thing. Chaz had been the Scarecrow, Lawrence, her brother, the Tin Man, her dog was Toto, and Chaz's dog was the Cowardly Lion. Only, as if he understood his role and wasn't happy about being labeled a coward, the ornery beagle had wriggled out of his lion mane and hidden it in his doghouse before they'd even started trick-or-treating.

As for the rest…well, of course Sarah had been Dorothy and Lulu had been the Wicked Witch of the West. Complete with green flour paste all over her face, a scraggly wig, horrific hat and butt-ugly dress. Not exactly the Posh Spice she'd pictured.

She was pretty sure Sarah was the one who'd gotten raisins in place of chocolate bars that year. Hell, maybe all of them had.

"One thing's for sure, I don't ever remember witches wearing black leather bustiers," he said.

"Or spider-web patterned tights?" she said with an eyebrow wag. She *so* loved the tights.

"The skirt and those heels don't hurt, either."

Yeah, most witches probably didn't wear flouncy, lacy black miniskirts, or screw-me shoes with silver chains around the ankles. All of which she'd donned to attract a guy who now held absolutely no interest for her, and which had instead drawn the eye of one she'd known forever, but had never really allowed herself to *see* until now. Strange, strange world.

"Back to the point. I noticed you, and then you smiled at me."

Yes, she had. A big, friendly, please-don't-figure-out-what-I've-been-thinking smile. "So I did."

"You have an *amazing* smile. Welcoming and uninhibited."

His tone was sincere, his eyes gleaming with something she couldn't quite place. Tenderness? Maybe that. Chaz had always had a nice, tender streak, which other kids had tried to crush. Her included, on occasion.

"When I saw that gorgeous smile, and realized it was directed at me, I figured you felt it, too."

"Felt what?" Right now all she felt was dazed by words she'd never expected to hear from *him* of all people.

He lifted a hand and dragged it through a long strand of her glittery, red-dyed hair, rubbing it lightly, then twining it in his fingers. "Attraction. Heat."

His bluntness shocked her. "Are you serious?"

"Completely."

She couldn't speak, honestly could not find a word to say.

"I've surprised you again?"

Nodding slowly, she admitted, "Just a bit."

"Sorry. I've been out of the country too long. I've lost my manners and forgotten how this game's supposed to be played."

"Are we playing a game?"

"Oh, yeah."

He breathed deeply to inhale the scent of her hair, and lightly, oh, so lightly, kissed her temple, just above the edge of the mask.

She managed to stay upright at this first-ever kiss between them, even though worlds rocked and tides changed and planets skipped out of orbit at the brush of his lips on her skin.

Every instinct she owned was telling her that this wasn't Chaz, that he'd been replaced by a doppelgänger who didn't hate her, who saw her as the sensual woman she'd become and not the mean-spirited kid he'd once known. What other explanation was there? A dream?

This is really happening, isn't it?

"What kind of game?" she finally asked.

Another brush of soft lips on her pulse point, then he inhaled deeply, as if imprinting her scent on his memory. "The kind that ends with us in bed."

"Holy shit."

He laughed. "Shocked you that time, huh?"

"Oh, *hell* yes."

"Sorry. It's just been a long while since I've been with anyone. A long time since I've wanted to, to be perfectly honest. And the minute I saw that smile, I just…wanted you."

How on earth could this sexy, forthright, demanding guy have been born out of the shy, nerdy boy she'd known?

"I know it's quick, and it's crazy. I don't usually do this. Actually, I don't think I've ever moved so fast with a woman in my life. But the truth is, I want to take you out of here and have sex with you like the sun's not gonna come up tomorrow."

Whoa.

This time, she couldn't keep her feet steady. Her ankle twisted and she stumbled in the attractive-but-misera-bly-uncomfortable high heels. If he hadn't had his arms wrapped around her, she would have fallen right at his feet.

"Okay, point taken. I'm going too fast," he said as he held her tightly against him, so she could feel every rope of muscle, each ounce of masculinity. Including a ridge in his pants that said he was not in any way, shape, or form a boy. He was all, total, 100 percent powerful man.

"Fast? You could be in a car commercial about going from zero to one-twenty in ten seconds flat."

"Sorry," he said with an I'm-not-really-sorry shrug. "Let's back up, play this the normal way, with introductions. I'm not mysterious like the guitarist. My name's Chaz. What's yours?"

Gasping, she stumbled over her own feet again. Chaz tightened his grip on her hips, preventing her weak, suddenly trembling legs from giving out on her. Her head spun, her thoughts pinging around like a ball in a pinball machine until the reality settled in and became something she believed.

Son of a bitch.

"My...my name?"

"Yeah. You have one, don't you?"

She nodded, her brain still scrambling.

He didn't recognize her. Chaz Browning had no idea who she was. That's why he could make those suggestive comments to her—he had no clue he'd been making them to the girl he'd grown up with!

The truth of it settled in, and she went over the past several minutes in her mind. He'd seen her, noting the costume, and of course the mask that covered two-thirds of her face. But he hadn't recognized *her,* Lulu, the bane of his childhood.

Actually, it did make sense. It was stupid of her to think he would have recognized her at a glance, across a crowded bar, after nine years. He'd remember her as a kid, and right now she was wearing a very sexy costume, and her hair was red and curly. Why on earth would he have known her?

She should have realized that. In her own defense, she could only say she hadn't been thinking clearly, she'd been too affected by the grown-up version of the boy she'd known. She was still affected by him, in fact, and growing more so by the minute.

"How potent are those red drinks?" he asked, laughter in his voice. "If they induce amnesia, they should come with a warning label."

"Pretty potent."

She smiled weakly as the truth of the situation continued to settle in to all the most adventurous parts of her brain. A world of possibilities opened up like a long road at the start of an exciting journey. She was a stranger to him. Just a sexy stranger, a hot woman Chaz Browning was trying to pick up.

And, although an hour ago she'd never have dreamed it possible, she was seriously considering letting him.

"Umm…let's hold off on the name thing for a while."

His eyes widened as if he thought she was kidding. When he realized she wasn't, he shrugged. "If you say so."

She did say so, because she was still trying to figure things out. Things like how much she wanted him. Whether she could have him.

Despite the obstacles—their careers, her bratty past that had to have left him hating her, their siblings' angry relationship, their parents' lifelong friendship, and all the stolen candy bars and broken tailbones history that said they could never make a relationship work—she found herself wanting him more than she'd ever wanted a man in her life.

Her curiosity ate at her, of course, and the attraction had been instantaneous. But it was more than that. She had known him as a child, and she greatly wanted to know him as a man. Would the sparks they'd shot off each other throughout their lives transition into a different kind of heat altogether?

Just once, for one wild night, could she have him? Take him, be with him, get the longing and the ache out of her system and then go back to being his friend/enemy without hurting anyone or letting things get complicated? Was that possible?

Catwoman and Batman managed it.

Sure. Nemeses to lovers worked sometimes, if only in the short run. Maybe it wasn't smart, but it was at least possible.

It also sounded very exciting.

There was just one problem. It *had* to be in the short run. There was no way they could have any kind of future, not with all the baggage and the family issues. Besides, he was an internationally traveling reporter—and she intended to stay right here and change the world in other ways.

Meaning if something happened between them, it had to be a one-shot deal. Something with no drama, no angsting, no questions even.

Which meant Chaz could never know the truth.

If she slept with him tonight, she had to make damn sure he never found out who she actually was. And that meant she had to stay in control.

2

CHAZ HAD MET plenty of beautiful women before.

He'd traveled all over the world covering stories of glamorous spies, interacting with powerful politicians and sexy stars. He'd had a few more lovers than a nice small-town-boy should probably ever admit to having. He'd been in love once, infatuated twice, and in lust dozens of times. But he'd never felt his heart stop beating in his chest at the sight of a woman's smile.

Until tonight. Until her.

This stranger, this redhead with a half mask that made her dark eyes gleam nearly black, had a smile that could stop the world on its axis. Her amazing body and mysteriously beautiful face had caught his eye the minute he'd entered. But that smile…nations could rise or fall on a smile like that. And now, having her in his arms, he knew there wasn't much he wouldn't give to make sure this night ended just as he'd told her he wanted it to. Whether he ever learned her name or not.

"Penny for your thoughts?" he asked when she settled back into his arms, her clumsiness an adorable indicator that she was interested, maybe even turned on, by his suggestive comments.

The music changed, the torchy song swinging into something a little faster, but neither of them separated. They continued the sexy, sultry glide of hip to hip, thigh on thigh.

"My thoughts'll cost you a nickel," she said, her voice a bit deeper, throatier than before. As if she was intentionally ratcheting up the flirtation level. She'd gone from sweet to sexy, if only in her tone.

"Inflation sucks."

"Okay, the first one's free. One of the things I was thinking is that I should thank you for preventing me from falling on my ass in front of all of these people."

"Those are some dangerous shoes you're wearing."

"It's not the shoes," she admitted.

"So, it's the company?"

"More like the conversation."

"Should I apologize?"

She snagged a lush lower lip between her teeth, and slowly shook her head. "No. Please don't. I like a man who says what's really on his mind. That's pretty rare."

"Especially in this city. Honesty is a lost art here."

She glanced down toward the floor, toward those oh-so-sexy shoes with the silver chains that resembled handcuffs. Damn, the moment he'd spotted them, they'd put some seriously wicked ideas in his head.

Lately, he'd been living in a high-adrenaline, high-risk zone. People in those situations couldn't hesitate to take risks, even though they never knew what dangers might be lurking around the corner. He apparently hadn't gotten out of that mindset—out of the need to go for what you wanted the moment you spotted it, because you might not get another chance.

Maybe if he'd met her a week from now, he'd never have

told this beautiful stranger what he was really thinking. Maybe as soon as tomorrow, he'd regret having done it.

At this moment, though, looking at her luscious mouth and losing himself in those dark, deep-set eyes, he didn't regret a damn thing.

"Are you really not going to give me your name?"

She hesitated.

"Do I have to pay for that, too? I'm not sure I have enough nickels. Or any American money at all, to be honest."

"So I take it I'm buying the first round?"

"Maybe we can go somewhere else where the drinks are cheaper," he said, staring intently into her dark eyes, wishing he could see her whole face without the admittedly sensual mask.

There was something erotic about her anonymity. He had no doubt she was beautiful beneath the mask, but couldn't deny the anticipation of removing it was exciting.

"Where did you have in mind?"

"I live a couple of blocks from here."

She licked those lips, sending another sharp stab of lust surging through him. Damn, the woman was getting to him with every single breath she took. He'd been sexually on edge since he'd left for his trip a few months ago, and certainly hadn't had any relief during it. Now, knowing her all of fifteen minutes, he was ready to rip her sexy bustier open, yank her skirt off, and explore every delicious inch of her.

"That's certainly something to keep in mind," she said. "But didn't you say we were backing up? I think you're directionally challenged. That was pretty forward."

He laughed, enjoying her bluntness, her humor. She was refreshing, challenging and sharp. He was starting to like her as well as want her.

"Okay. Sorry. Backing up." The music changed, and he said, "Want to go grab a drink? At the bar, not at my place."

She nodded and let him lead her toward the bar. He shouldered his way in, calling their drink orders to one of the harried-looking bartenders.

"Do you need money?" she asked.

He shook his head. "I was kidding. I can cover it."

She stuck out her hand. "Okay, then, where's my nickel?"

Laughing, enjoying everything about her, he dug a coin out of his pocket and dropped it into her hand.

"Ahh, the beautiful feel of cold hard nickels."

Drinks in hand, he led her away from the table where she'd been sitting with her friends. No way did he want to sit with the shark who'd eyed him like he was chum. He had to wonder what this woman had been doing with somebody like that, since she didn't seem at all on-the-make as her dark-haired friend did, or, actually, as innocent as the lighter-haired one seemed.

His witch was just right.

Heading toward a small empty high-top in the corner, he put their drinks on it, and then helped her hop up onto a stool. She crossed one leg over the other. The position revealed a devastatingly sexy length of thigh, and he swallowed hard as he took his seat opposite her.

He sipped the drink, having gotten the special for himself, and grimaced. "Yeah. Cough syrup."

"I warned ya."

"I had to try one holiday-themed drink, and the only other choice was some green, glow-in-the-dark ectoplasm stuff."

They talked drinks for a few minutes, and then music. He realized they had very similar tastes. She was a great conversationalist, but he would never remember half of what she said. He just lost himself staring at her and listening to that sexy, throaty voice—which occasionally tipped up into a more normal tone, one that seemed familiar to him somehow. He was about to ask if she had a cold, or if she'd been around a smoker, but she asked him something first.

"So, Chaz, why were you overseas?" she asked, taking over the conversation. That was a good thing, since he wasn't sure he'd be able to think of anything except how much he was dying to taste that vulnerable spot on the hollow of her throat.

Besides, it was better than *Nice weather we're having*.

"I'm a journalist. I was following a story in Pakistan and ended up staying in Islamabad to help with a new media outfit."

"That sounds exciting."

"It can be. Some days are just routine, but the situation there is just so…unsettled." *Well, that's the understatement of the night.*

"So I hear."

Remembering some of the darker parts of his trip—the things he'd seen and wished he could forget—he admitted, "It's a completely different world."

One where he'd witnessed some of the worst—but also, he had to concede, some of the best—of humanity. Dirt and poverty warred with decency and a strong desire for a better life. He'd met people he would consider good friends… and others to whom he would never have turned his back for fear of them sticking a knife in it. It had been like living on a high wire for two months, but, quite honestly, it was what he lived for. He'd always hated liars as a kid, and now he got to bring down the biggest and worst all over the world. Still, it was exhausting, and he was glad to be back in the U.S. of A. Particularly at the start of the whole holiday season. His parents hadn't expected him home for Thanksgiving and he looked forward to calling them tomorrow to tell them he'd be there.

"Were you in real danger?"

"I never really felt like it, except the two times I crossed over into Afghanistan. Things got a little hairy on the second trip."

She gasped. "Are you crazy? How could you take a risk like that?"

"Chasing a story," he said, amused at her response. She'd reacted as though she were a disapproving family member rather than a woman he'd just met. "Believe me, there wasn't a minute when I wasn't aware of my surroundings."

"Your family must not have been happy about your being there."

That inspired a brief laugh. "You think I'm insane? I didn't tell them!"

He'd swear she was frowning in disapproval beneath that mask. "Maybe it's good you didn't. I'm sure your parents would have been terrified for you."

"Yes, they would have," he said, wondering if she, too, had overprotective parents. "That's why I didn't say anything to them. The trips were in-and-out, neither lasting longer than thirty-six hours. No point in worrying anybody when I was so far away and nothing they could have said would have changed my mind about going anyway."

"I read about some journalists who were attacked there last spring."

His hand tightened around his glass, an instinctive reaction, and a familiar pang of sorrow stabbed him in the gut. "Yes, I knew one of them. She was a wonderful photojournalist." Her death had been part of what made him so conscious of his surroundings for every second of the trip—and so determined to keep doing what he was doing.

Maybe that was also one reason why he was being a little reckless tonight. He'd been tense for weeks, he needed to let loose, shake off the last vestiges of emotional darkness, be around someone exciting and daring. Someone like *her*.

"All I can say is it's great to be home where…"

"Where you can proposition a sexy stranger?"

He smiled, incredibly grateful that she'd lightened the mood again. It was as if she'd read his mind and understood he'd gone as far as he wanted to go on the memory-lane trip.

"Uh-oh, I think you were the one who stepped forward that time."

"Sideways, maybe. The question was related to the subject at hand."

"So it was." He tossed back the rest of his drink, stood, and offered her his hand. "Let's dance again."

She immediately rose, twining her soft fingers with his. He squeezed lightly, wondering why he had such a sudden, shocking feeling of rightness at it being there. Funny, how quickly she was affecting him.

They were back on the dance floor, swaying to another bluesy Halloweenish song, when he remembered what she'd said back at the table. "So, you think you're sexy, do you?"

"I think *you* think I am."

Sexy enough to stop his heart. "Oh? You seem pretty self-assured."

"Well, you gave me a hint with your have-sex-like-the-sun-isn't-gonna-come-up-tomorrow line."

"That wasn't a line," he said, his voice steady, resolute. "It was a promise."

She wobbled again. Damn, he loved rocking her out of her spike-heeled shoes that were more of a sexual invitation than a foot covering.

"Now who's the self-assured one?" she whispered.

"I guess that makes us a good pair."

"I wasn't the one who made suggestive comments about suns not rising."

"But you didn't slap my face and walk away, either."

"No, I didn't."

She lifted her chin and squared her shoulders, so obviously trying to regain the upper hand, he almost laughed. "So, the whole sun-not-coming-up thing. What does it mean, anyway? Aside from the obvious."

He quirked a brow. "Huh?"

"Why would the sun not coming up make the sex better? Is it because it would go on so long since the night would never end?"

She tried to sound arch and noncommittal, but he could already read this woman very well. Part of her was urging him on, another trying to throw up artificial barriers to buy herself time to figure out where on earth they were going with this attraction.

"Or do you need to be in the dark?" She gasped a little, the sound over-exaggerated. "Are you...deformed in some way?"

"Wicked witch coming out to play?" he said with a lazy grin, not letting her get the rise out of him she was trying to.

"Do you like her?"

"A lot."

"Maybe you haven't seen her at her wickedest yet."

He couldn't make it out entirely, but he'd swear he could see a twinkle in those dark, mask-encircled eyes. She was teasing him. Daring him. *Two steps forward again.*

"I look forward to it. To answer your question, I have no problem in the light or the dark. I'm quite comfortable getting naked and utterly wild in broad daylight."

She quivered the tiniest bit before replying, "You certainly did put on a show here."

He tilted his head to the side, curious as to what she meant.

"When you were taking off your sheet, you pulled your shirt almost all the way off." Wagging an index finger at him, she said, "You had to have noticed. Were you just showing off that back and those shoulders?"

He barked a loud laugh, hearing the compliment hidden within the complaint. "I swear, I didn't realize it right away."

She harrumphed. "Well, every woman in the place did."

Including her. How nice.

"By the way," he said, remembering he'd never answered her question, not surprising given the strange turns they'd taken in this twisty conversation, "I was thinking more along the lines of last-night-on-earth sex."

Her brow furrowed, then she realized what he was talking about. "Ah. We're back to the sun not coming up?"

"Right." Wondering if she would notice his own determined eye twinkle, he took the charm up a notch. "You know, the world's gonna end, you have a few hours left, how else do you spend it?"

"Catching up on *The Walking Dead?* Eating pizza?" *Step back.*

He didn't let her distract him. *Forward. Like dancing.* "I was thinking more along the lines of lying naked in someone's arms."

Another flick of that pretty pink tongue on her lush lips.

She remained silent, not moving in either direction.

So he verbally advanced again…and again.

"Touching, tasting, exploring every erotic possibility. Giving and receiving so much pleasure, the experience leaves a mark on the world that lasts through the end of time."

"Well, I suppose that sounds better than zombies."

"Thanks."

She pulled her hand away and smoothed her hair, lifting it off her neck as if she'd suddenly gotten very hot. Still, she tried her best to regain control. "You know, that mark on the world wouldn't last very long if the world was ending."

Jesus, the woman was killing him here. He couldn't guess which witch he was going to get from one moment to the next. Not that it mattered. He just wanted to kiss her, to screw her, to laugh with her.

"I was speaking metaphorically. I'm a writer. Sue me."

"Do you really think the earth would end if the sun didn't come up?" she asked. "I mean, just to clarify, I realize you're a writer, not a scientist, but it's possible something would survive to…"

He cut her off. "I don't care. I just know the earth might end if I don't get to kiss you soon."

She giggled.

"Cheesy?"

"Maybe a little."

"How's this? If you don't come home with me and let me fuck your brains out tonight, I might never get over it."

Those beautiful lips parted and she breathed across them, breathy sighs in every exhalation. She stared up at him, searchingly, questioningly, and he never broke the stare, letting her see he didn't regret the words and truly meant them.

"You surprise me more and more, Chaz."

"In a good way?"

A slow, deliberate nod as she assessed him, brown eyes glowing. "Definitely. And FYI, I don't think I'd ever get over it, either."

Oh, thank God.

They danced a little more, but now a thick, sexual silence built between them, surging louder and hotter as the music underscored everything they'd said, everything they'd fantasized, everything they wanted. He had no doubt she was thinking the same thing he was—about getting out of here, being alone somewhere. He couldn't wait to find out if these incredible sparks they shot off each other would start a blaze with their first real kiss and become volcanic in bed.

The music shifted again, this time to a faster song that didn't necessitate slow dancing. Both of them ignored that, though, and kept close, swaying, thrusting, mindless and silent. Every brush of her body against his, every shared breath, every stroke of his fingers against the small of her back or press of his thigh against hers was heightening things to ever more intense levels. Her hands did wild and wicked things, riding low on his hips. She kissed his throat, scraping her teeth along his collarbone, which made him groan lightly and repay her in kind until the groan was hers.

Finally, she stopped moving and inched away from him. She distanced herself enough to suck in a few deep, calming, audible breaths. Her lips were full, swollen, her eyes luminous behind the mask. Her whole body was pink and flushed. Her nipples were pebbled, visible even beneath the sexy bustier. A warm, womanly scent rose from her, filling his head, making his mouth water and his brain fog as he realized just how aroused she had become.

Other people on the floor merely moved around them, grinning, casting knowing looks, aware he and his mystery woman had been all but having sex in the middle of the crowd. He'd bet they weren't the only ones.

"Are you okay?" he asked. He wondered if she'd drag him out the door, which was what he most wanted her to do. He mentally held his breath, waiting for her to decide.

"I was getting overheated," she said.

"I noticed," he said, realizing if she listened hard enough, she wouldn't hear teasing, but pure, utter desire in his words.

A long pause. A longer stare.

"I feel like I've known you forever," he admitted, wondering why everything about her appealed to him so deeply.

Wrong thing to say, apparently. She stiffened the tiniest bit. And back she stepped.

"I, uh…look, it's a holiday, we might be acting out of character. I don't want either of us to do anything we might someday regret." Her breaths had slowed, her color returning to normal. "So let's maybe just stay here for a while longer?"

As if he would ever regret making love to this woman? Fat chance. Of course, he'd only met her an hour ago, so he supposed she had a right to slow things down. Again.

He found himself enjoying their sexual dance, the push-and-pull, back-and-forth, a lot. The chase was building his excitement, lifting the anticipation until it hung around them like a vapor.

"I understand. I like dancing with you."

Her relieved sigh told him she'd been holding her breath physically as well as mentally, waiting to see if he was going to agree to cool off or keep up the flirtation.

"Thanks," she said, moving into his arms again, though he noticed she kept an inch or two of overheated air between their bodies. "Believe me, I'm not a cock-tease. It's just…I don't want either of us to have any regrets."

"I won't," he said, meaning it.

Chaz couldn't help wondering what was making her so skittish. She was hot and sexy one moment, funny and chatty the next. He liked both personalities, but it was the hot and sexy one he wanted to spend the night with. Still, he already suspected he wanted to have breakfast with funny and chatty.

He supposed he wasn't thinking about this in the typical-guy one-night-stand way. Chaz had had a few of those—quick lays, hurried goodbyes before the sun rose, scarcely another thought about the encounter. They were perils of a job that required him to travel a lot, rarely leaving him time to settle down and really get to know someone.

Now, though, he would be stateside for a while, possibly. And within hours of getting here, he'd found someone he really did want to get to know. While he could have taken it slow and played the dating game, the night was too wild, their connection too immediate and his desire for her too insistent. But that didn't mean one night was all he wanted.

Besides, he didn't know her name, and hadn't really seen her face yet. No way was he going to let her get away tonight without being sure of both. The woman could hardly hide behind a mask if they spent the whole night engaged in hot, steamy sex. As for her name and number, he'd kiss the info right off her lips if it was the last thing he ever did.

Whatever the name, he could at least try to start solving the mystery of her identity. "So, what about you? What do you do for a living?"

She relaxed in his arms. "I work for a nonprofit group

providing microloans to single mothers in third-world countries."

"I've heard of those organizations," he said, trying to recall the details. "I actually talked to someone about that recently. Can't remember who."

Her throat worked visibly as she swallowed, and he felt her tension rise again "Well, it's a great cause," she said quietly. "But surely not as exciting as what you do."

"It's not about the excitement. Someone needs to hold these liars and fraudsters accountable. Just because they have power, or money or a 'good reason' doesn't excuse the damage they do."

She blanched and he realized he'd gone too far. "Sorry, I get a little wound up. I've been told I have 'trust issues.'"

"I can understand that, after what happened to your friend. Maybe we shouldn't talk shop."

"Okay, no work stuff. So, are you ready to give me your name?"

"Let's say I prefer to be a woman of mystery tonight."

He frowned.

"Is that a deal-breaker?"

He considered it, already suspecting one night with her wouldn't be enough. He'd definitely want to know how to reach her later. But the night was young, and if it ended up where he hoped it would, she'd still be in his arms in the morning. There would be time for details, he had no doubt. For now, the pulsating music, the eroticism of her sultry voice, the lights shining on her red hair, the blood-red remnants of her drink on her lips, the innate hunger... they were enough. Most definitely.

"No. Not a deal-breaker. I doubt you could say anything that would be."

One corner of her sexy mouth curved up in a tiny smile, and she gave a throaty chuckle. "Never say never."

Something came to mind. "You're not married, right?"

"Completely unattached."

He released the breath he hadn't realized he'd been holding. "Good."

"You?" she asked.

"Nope. I've been told I'm not marriage material."

She sneered. "Told by some woman who wanted you to commit before you were ready?"

"That's pretty perceptive."

"It's in the female phrasebook."

"I need to get one of those."

"That'll cost you more than a nickel. State secrets and all."

"I should already have one, considering I had a bunch of girls around growing up."

She stiffened slightly in his arms.

"Is family a touchy subject we are supposed to avoid, like witches and going back to my place for a drink?"

"No. I'm just picturing you as a kid."

"Don't bother. I was a born loser."

"I don't believe that," she said, suddenly vehement.

"If the word 'geek' is in that handbook of yours, my picture's beside it."

"Well, I bet the girls you grew up with feel pretty stupid now," she whispered.

"I doubt it," he replied, remembering his gawkiest years, when he'd been a skinny, uncoordinated sad-sack. "They wouldn't recognize me if they fell over me today."

She mumbled something that he couldn't catch—something like *I know what you mean*—which was interesting. Because he had a hard time picturing her ever being anything but gorgeous, and she was unforgettable. He would *never* forget that smile.

"It's all right," he told her. "Believe me, I'm not carrying around any angst from my childhood. Though, I do avoid going back to my small hometown as much as possible."

She cleared her throat. "You never go home to see your family because of the way other kids treated you?"

"Nah. I go once in a while, not for a few years, though. I'm busy traveling. My parents meet up with me sometimes—last year they came to Berlin when I was on assignment. And I should see my kid sister more now since she just started grad school here in D.C. this semester."

"Your sister is in the city?" She nibbled her lip. "Where does she go to school?"

"Sarah goes to American University."

She stopped dancing. "So does La…um, so does somebody I know. Small world."

"Yeah," he said, meaning it. He'd traveled enough of it to know. "Can we be done talking about our childhoods and our families now?"

"Oh, yes, please!"

"Good. Let's get back to discussing how red your lips are."

"Were we discussing that?"

"If we weren't, we should have been."

Her tongue flicked out and moistened those sensual lips, and he had to clench his teeth as the temperature went up another ten degrees.

"I wasn't lying. I am going to have to kiss you soon."

Her throat visibly worked as she swallowed. "Are you asking me or telling me?"

"Does it matter?"

He didn't give her a chance to answer; he couldn't wait anymore. Those red lips were driving him crazy, and he had to taste her or go completely mental right here on the dance floor. So without warning, he bent and caught her mouth with his. Her lips parted right away, warm, hungry and welcoming, and he kissed her deeply, tasting cherry, whiskey and woman.

She wrapped her arms around his neck, holding him tight, tilting her head and pressing even closer. Her tongue swept against his, thrusting, demanding, and he answered every thrust, each demand. She was sweet and hot, and every cell in his body came to attention, all electricity, fire and need.

Their heartbeats matched, racing, and the kiss went deeper, hotter, wetter. He sunk his hands into her thick, curling hair, and she grabbed his hips, tugging him hard against her, until his hardening cock was nestled low against her belly. They were surrounded in the club, but he didn't give a damn. He felt as though he needed her mouth to provide the very air in his lungs. Kissing her was like diving head first into a deep well filled with nothing but pleasure and excitement, and he had to forcibly pull his mouth away when he realized they were soon going to reach the point where it would be too agonizing to stop.

When it finally ended, they remained close, his forehead pressed against hers, both of them panting. He was rock-hard against her and she ground against him instinctively, as if her body had already made the decision she hadn't yet voiced.

"You ready to go get that drink at my place?" he asked, hearing the hoarse need in his own voice.

If she said no, he might just have to go into the bathroom and jerk off. If she said yes, he wasn't sure he'd be able to make it across the room and out the door without putting a bag over his crotch.

"I don't usually do this," she said, as if worried he might think less of her. But how could he, when he was barely capable of thought at all?

"Honestly? Neither do I."

"So we're both feeling reckless tonight?"

He scraped his knuckles against her jaw, brushing his thumb over her well-kissed lips. "Maybe it's because there's just magic and madness in the air."

"You might be right," she said, smiling up at him as she twined her fingers in his hair. "Whatever the reason...yes, Chaz, I am ready to go get that drink."

3

LULU DIDN'T QUESTION her decision or second-guess herself. She simply laced her fingers with Chaz's, and let him lead her back over to her table so she could grab her things and say good-night. Viv had gone to the dance floor and was gyrating in the middle of a mosh pile of guys, and Amelia was talking to someone at the next table. As Lulu grabbed her purse and coat, Amelia raised a curious eyebrow but didn't ask any questions, merely wishing her a Happy Halloween and smiling at Chaz. Blessing the more tactful of her two friends, she let Chaz drag her out of the bar, both of them desperate to find someplace to be alone.

Lulu wasn't going to allow herself to think about how crazy this was. Nor could she dwell on how their families might react. She suspected all four parents would like the idea of the two of them together romantically, but they probably wouldn't love the whole one-night-stand thing, which was all this was going to be.

Hell, she couldn't even imagine how Chaz himself would react if he knew who she was! She was just going to do it—take something she wanted, and then let it go, content with the memories of an amazing experience that would be her secret forever more.

They got outside and the sharp October air filled her lungs, redolent with the scent of a log fire burning nearby. Everything about the night revealed the pleasures of autumn—a season she'd missed when going to college and grad school in Arizona. Dry leaves rustled on the trees and blew gently across the sidewalks. The stars filling the sky weren't too dimmed by the city lights, and the air was cold enough so little puffs were visible when they exhaled.

Dupont Circle was an area popular with people her age—young professionals, new grads, maybe a few families, but certainly none were out this late for any candy-begging. Inside every bar and coffeehouse, though, loud music played and voices could be heard even through closed doors. Few lingered on the streets. By now, folks in costume had arrived at their preferred holiday destinations and were staying inside, as an early cold snap had made D.C. a chilly place to be outside at this time of night.

"It's a perfect night for being wicked," she said, keeping her voice low, thick and throaty, as she'd tried to do once she'd realized he didn't know who she was. She might very well see him as herself in a few days and did not want to make herself so easily recognizable.

"I agree. I'm planning all kinds of wickedness with you."

"Are you sure you're not interested in candy corn anymore?" she asked with a flirtatious grin. "You could always try to find an all-night convenience store."

"Definitely not," he replied, dropping an arm across her shoulders, tugging her tightly against his body as they walked. "I wouldn't walk away from you right now if sweet old Lady Larsen from my hometown showed up with a whole box of Snickers bars."

A giggle escaped her lips but she quickly silenced it. As a stranger, she shouldn't know about old Lady Larsen, a neighbor of theirs when they'd grown up. She'd always given out full-size candy bars on Halloween. Every kid in town had hit her house.

"How far away is your place?" she asked, to cover her near-miss.

"Just a couple of blocks away," said Chaz.

Lulu already knew that. When his real estate agent had shown her the available rental properties around here, she'd pointed out the cute townhouse Chaz had bought last year. It was a couple of doors down from the carved-up brownstone in which Lulu had an apartment. They were almost as neighborly as they'd been growing up. Yikes.

That would make things very uncomfortable if he found out who she was, but should also make her getaway easier tonight.

"Will you be okay walking there in those shoes?" he asked, staring down at her feet with a frown.

"I'll be fine," she insisted, ready to run if it meant they could be alone and could get back to that crazy-wild-delicious kissing. And everything that came after it.

She'd walked to the bar, too. But she didn't reveal that, not wanting to let on that she lived around here. She was already being very careful, unwilling to leave him too many clues.

Of course, she might be overestimating her own sexual potency. Maybe tonight would be forgettable, and Chaz would never again wonder about the red-haired, green-masked witch he'd seduced on Halloween night. But she doubted it. Their chemistry was strong. She suspected the encounter would be something they'd both long remember.

"I'm glad it's close," she said. "I don't want to wait too long for that wickedness you promised."

They'd walked for less than a minute, hadn't even rounded the corner to turn onto his—their—street, but

Chaz pulled her off the sidewalk into the shadows beside a credit-union building. "You don't have to wait another second."

She threw her arms around his neck and tugged him to her, parting her lips before they met his. They tasted each other as thoroughly as they had on the dance floor, but this was slower, less frantic, more erotic. The pulsing, seething hunger was there, but, as if they both knew it would soon be satisfied, they were content to kiss like pleasure-seeking lovers and not like strangers trying to figure out if one kiss was all they'd have.

Sharing merely one kiss with Chaz would have been a crime for the ages, she realized as he cupped her face in his hands and tilted his head. Their tongues danced. He swallowed down her sighs, tasting her, teasing her. His subtle cologne wafted to her nostrils and she went softer and wetter as the scent imprinted a sense memory in her, one she knew she would recall forever when she smelled his fragrance.

She couldn't wait to touch him. Remembering how easily the shirt had glided over that incredible body, she slid her hands around his lean hips, and pushed up. The shirt moved with her fingers, leaving her free to explore that hot male flesh. His body rippled with muscle, and was slick with desire-stoked sweat. She touched him, explored him, wanting to taste her way along every ridge and line.

"Christ," he mumbled against her mouth when she scraped her nails across his bare back.

Inflamed, he picked her up by the waist, wrapping her legs around his hips and supporting her entire weight. He swung around, bracing her against the building, kissing her more desperately. One big, powerful hand stroked the outside of her thigh, pushing up under the skirt.

The heat and friction of his fingers against the patterned

tights heightened her awareness. She was conscious of every single sensation battering at her senses. Being completely in his control, held by him, explored by him, she closed her eyes and enjoyed it. Maybe it was the holiday, or the eroticism, or the drinks…something was making her lose every inhibition and give herself over to him and those magical hands.

Despite the possibility of discovery, he seemed unable to stop himself from touching her. Reaching up under her skirt and tugging at the waistband of her tights, he got them low enough to delve into.

"Naughty girl," he whispered against her mouth when he realized she wore no panties.

"Very naughty. Because right now, I wish the tights were crotchless," she admitted.

"I'd give a year off my life if they were," he said.

He made do by pulling the tights down a bit more, until he was holding her bare ass, stroking, squeezing.

"Mmm," she groaned, wanting more than anything for him to pull her legs even farther apart, opening her to him so he could slam into her right now.

He lifted her higher, shocking her with his strength. Long gone was the uncoordinated, weak little kid. She wondered if he now liked to pick up cars in his spare time.

Holding on to her with one arm, he began a determined, erotic exploration with his other hand. He pushed the tights down farther, until he could slide his hand between her cheeks. He touched her intimately, the sensations wickedly erotic, making her gasp with shocked pleasure. Her gasps turned into needy pleas as his fingers moved deeper, reaching the curls covering her sex and tangling in them. Lulu arched eagerly toward the touch, wanting everything and more from him.

"I wanna drop to my knees and bury my face here,"

he said, his need making him handle her roughly, clenching her so tightly she'd probably have bruises tomorrow.

She didn't care, wanting him as hot and crazed and out-of-his-mind as he was making her.

"Yes, oh please," she groaned, wanting him to move those fingers just a tiny bit more so he could slip one inside her.

He shifted her to try to grant her unspoken wish, but the rough brick of the building scraped her hip, scratching her sharply. Lulu hissed in pain.

"Oh, God, I'm sorry." He immediately pulled her away from the wall, still holding her tightly, her legs around his hips. "I wouldn't hurt that magnificent ass for anything—not when all I want to do is nibble it."

"I'm not sorry," she said, pressing frantic kisses on his mouth. "It's worth it, and you can nibble away." Feeling the cold air against her exposed bottom, she giggled. "Though it *is* a little cold."

"I guess we should go."

"Just get me to the nearest warm place and finish what you started," she urged, not sure she'd have the patience to walk blocks at this point. Nor that her legs would carry her.

Chaz turned to glance around. If a seedy, rent-by-the-room hotel had been across the street, she would have raced him to it, but no such luck.

Still, a smile crossed his lips. Lulu followed his stare, seeing his gaze had landed on the door of the credit union. It had an after-hours key-card lock for customers to use the ATM in the vestibule. He studied it for a moment, then looked at her and lifted a suggestive brow.

"You wouldn't dare," she said, her tone amused and a little taunting. Was she egging him on? She honestly wasn't sure.

"Watch me."

"A *camera* will be watching you."

He glanced back toward the bar they'd left. "Damn. I forgot my sheet. We can't be unidentifiable ghost and witch."

"You would pull a sheet over us, take me in there and...?"

"Oh, hell yes. Right this very minute." He edged closer to the door. "Of course, maybe we don't need the sheet. If we're very careful, and you keep your mask on...."

"Are you an exhibitionist?" she asked, half shocked, more than half aroused. The vestibule was fully exposed right inside the building, and fairly well lit. Though nobody was around to watch, there could be at any moment.

"Honestly, I don't give a flying fuck who sees us. I just want to touch you, get my fingers in you, see if you're as tight and wet as I think you are."

She had to close her eyes as more blood rerouted toward her sex. The man was intoxicating and aggressive, nothing like the boy she'd known, and his demands rang with sexual confidence.

"But there must be cameras," she said, her protest sounding weak to even her ears.

"There's just one in the machine, recording anybody right in front of it. It can't catch all the corners and sides."

"Are you sure?"

"I bank here. I'm pretty sure. But we can go in and check."

She felt herself weakening.

"Just a quick exploration," he begged, kissing her throat, then scraping the tip of his tongue down to the tops of her breasts. "Throw a starving man a bone so I'll have the strength to get us back to my place. I'll carry you home, just like this, and save you from those wicked shoes, if I can just take a tour of your delicious body right now."

She held on tight, her fingers digging into his shoulders as she urged him on. "Do it."

Letting her down, he grabbed her hand and pulled her with him to the front of the building. "I've never been more glad that I bank here," he said as he pulled out his wallet.

He removed his debit card, and swiped it in the card reader to unlock the door. She waited as he pulled it open and ushered her in. They were like fish in a bowl, encased in glass, visible to anyone lurking nearby.

She should have been shocked, nervous and ready to bolt. But the utter wickedness of it thrilled her. She hadn't done anything this daring for as long as she could remember, and the sheer riskiness of it urged her on almost as much as her hunger for him. She needed his hands on her, his mouth on her, but a part of her—the part that had been focused on school and work and hadn't spared a moment for sex—almost *wanted* to be seen.

She didn't spot a soul nearby, and they were surrounded by dark, closed businesses, but they were near lots of parked cars and were only a few buildings up from the bar they'd left.

And then there was the camera. She spotted it embedded in the top of the machine, pointing directly out to catch whoever was standing in front of the ATM. Chaz was already in line with it, and she had to be at least partly visible. No doubt they were already being recorded. But he was right about the tiny neighborhood bank's security. There were no other cameras in sight—no black domes on the ceiling or in the corners, just the one wired within the ATM, facing out, at about eye level.

They might really get away with this.

"Come here," Chaz ordered, beckoning her over. "Stand right there, with your back against the wall."

Understanding what he had in mind, she turned around

and backed into the corner directly beside the ATM. It couldn't possibly capture her image; she was side-by-side with the thing. And if there were any inside cameras, she was completely blocked from them by the interior wall between the vestibule and the lobby.

"I think I'll check my balance," Chaz said with a wicked grin as he inserted his card, eyeing her and not the screen.

"I suspect you've hit the jackpot," she teased.

He didn't even look over at her, exploring only by touch. Shifting slightly to further block the camera's view of his actions, he reached for her, scraping his fingers across her jaw, her lips, then tracing a line straight down her throat. She felt the touch down to her very toes, wishing his mouth would follow the same trajectory.

When he reached her bustier, he easily untied it, one-handed. She arched toward him, loving the brush of his warm skin against the sensitive curves. Drawing the laces, he loosened the whole top until it sagged open, and then, only then, did he glance away from the screen to stare at her.

"God almighty," he whispered, sounding nearly reverent. His eyes were dark with want. His muscles bunched under his shirt and his jaw clenched as he struggled to maintain control. Lulu had never seen a look of such pure, unadulterated want in anyone's face before.

She couldn't manage to say a thing as he reached for her breast, cupping it, squeezing gently, stroking his thumb over her hard, sensitized nipple. She was dying for his mouth, but he remained several inches away, pretending to focus only on the cash machine, while secretly pleasuring her just out of sight.

The man's patience stunned her; she was ready to say screw the camera and leap on him, pull his mouth to her breast and beg him to taste her. But he kept his cool, still blocking her from view of the camera, and from anyone who might walk up to the front of the vestibule.

The side, of course, was another story. She was looking right out into the parking lot, and if somebody approached from that way, they'd notice her standing inside, her top hanging open, her breasts freed and heavy, being caressed by a man who definitely knew how to use his hands.

"Damn, I forgot my pin number," he said with a chuckle. "You distracted me."

"Keep trying, you'll get it sooner or later," she whispered as she reached down and tugged her skirt up, inch by inch.

He shifted his gaze and watched, hunger dripping from him as he dropped his hand and stroked his way down her belly and between her legs. He cupped her sex and she arched into his touch, dying, spinning, flying, all at the same time. He felt so good, his touch so possessive, as if he were staking his claim to what lay beneath his hand.

"You're so hot."

"And getting hotter by the minute," she groaned.

"Show me."

He helped her tug the skirt the rest of the way up, and work her tights back down, baring herself from hips to upper thighs.

He couldn't seem to take his eyes off her. "You are gorgeous. I've got to get inside you."

"That might be difficult from that angle."

"My cock is just going to have to wait in line."

Her hips thrust reflexively. "Touch me. Please."

"Thanks, I think I will," he said, smiling wickedly as he again reached between her thighs.

He toyed with her clit for a moment, making the world tremble, bringing an orgasm to within tasting distance. While it rattled and thrummed through her, he slipped between the lips of her sex. She was drenched and ready, and his finger slid easily into her sensitive channel.

"Mmm," she said, closing her eyes and dropping her head back as he pleasured her.

"You are so tight. So wet for me."

"I got wet the minute you made that sun-coming-up comment."

"Thought it made you wonder if the world would end."

"I'm wondering that now—because if you don't make me come, I think it just might."

Masculine laughter rumbled from him as he moved his thumb to her clit and stroked it again. His long fingers pleasured her deep within, and his gentle swirling motion around her clit brought her up higher and higher, even as tension and stormy heat pooled lower and lower.

"Yes, Chaz," she groaned, torn between utter pleasure and a tension that was almost painful. She needed release desperately, and knew it was just a few breaths away.

As if sensing she was so close, he stepped over in front of her and caught her mouth in a hot kiss. Plunging his tongue deep, he stroked her right to the edge of the abyss, until she was almost sobbing against his lips.

"Please," she begged. "I need…oh, yes," she groaned as he gave her the right amount of pressure to send her soaring.

Her hips thrusting helplessly, Lulu gasped as waves of delight washed through her, to the top of her head, to the soles of her feet. Not one molecule was unaffected as she pulsed with satisfaction, and she wanted to cry at how good it felt. She couldn't remember coming so hard before in her entire life. If he could work such magic with his hand, she couldn't even fathom what he would do with his mouth, or with that powerful hard-on pressing against her middle.

Collapsing against him, still savoring his kiss, meeting every delicious thrust of his tongue, she tried to bring herself back down from the incredible high he'd provided.

Easing his lips from hers, he kissed his way down her throat, tasting her skin, sucking gently, biting lightly. He ended up at her breasts. Plumping one in his hand, he covered the tip with his mouth and sucked, hard. More heat sluiced through her, as if she hadn't just had a limb-weakening orgasm. Every inch of her that wasn't already on fire got that way immediately.

"These are beautiful," he told her, moving to pay attention to her other breast, suckling one nipple while he tweaked and caressed the other.

She kept her head back, her eyes closed, loving the moisture and heat of his lips and the stroke of his fingers. Her nipples were so sensitive, every pull of his mouth on her breast was echoed between her thighs. Her clit was pebble-hard again, and she was right on the edge of spilling into another climax.

"I think that's enough for now."

"You think so, do you?" she asked, twining her fingers in his hair.

"Yeah. That took the edge off. Let's let it build up again on the way back to my place."

Fiend. She was so wound up, that first orgasm might have happened a week ago.

Kissing his way up to her face, he stared down at her and gently helped her put her skirt and tights into place again. He left her bustier open so he could continue to play with her breasts, both building the pleasure and denying release with every firm yet gentle caress.

"Are you okay?"

"I'm not sure my legs work anymore."

"I promised I'd carry you. You held up your end of the bargain. I'll hold up mine."

She didn't doubt he could. Perhaps being a world-traveling adventurer equipped him to carry a girl for blocks down a dark, windswept street, after he'd fingered her into oblivion.

"Give me a sec to recover," she told him, not ready to go back out into the cold night and surrender their private—but oh-so-public—chamber. "Finish checking your balance."

He chuckled lightly. "I definitely can't remember my pin now. I'm not sure I can remember my name. That was something to see."

He looked as pleased and cocky as a man who'd made a woman come in under two minutes with just his fingers should look. And while it had been her pleasure to oblige him—most definitely—she also wanted him just as crazed and lost to sensual delight as she had been. "Maybe I can help you remember the number."

"Oh?"

"Sure. Go back over there and put your hands on the keys." She licked her lips. "And keep them there."

He didn't appear to understand at first, but he did as she ordered, stepping into place again and eyeing the machine. "Hmm. Deposit or withdrawal? Or just the balance check?"

"How about ninety minutes of serious deposits and withdrawals," she said. Her smile impish, she added, "Especially if you have a lot to deposit?"

"Find out for yourself."

Unable to wait, she did just that, reaching out to stroke the tented front of his pants. Feeling the massive erection straining against his zipper, she melted, the last bit of strength draining out of her legs. Sliding down the wall, she didn't stop until she sat on the backs of her calves.

Which was a very nice position to be in, indeed.

"What are you…"

"Let me see if I can help jog your memory, and, uh, take *your* edge off at the same time," she said, gazing up at him with wanton sweetness. "Maybe if you relax and don't think too hard about anything, the number will pop right into your mind."

He watched her, looking surprised and excited as she edged between him and the wall, directly below the machine, out of the camera's prying eye. Kneeling face-level with his groin, she grasped his zipper and carefully lowered it, her hand trembling as she acknowledged just how big he was.

"You aren't seriously…"

"Oh, yes, I am," she whispered, moving closer so she could brush her open mouth against the cotton of his tight boxer briefs. She exhaled and then pressed her tongue there, wetting the fabric, tasting the heat and musk of him.

"God almighty," he said, dropping a hand to tangle it in her hair. "Your mouth has been driving me crazy since the moment you smiled at me."

"Did you picture me using it on you…here?"

He groaned as she pressed her lips to the straining cotton again. "Not in the very first ten seconds after I saw you."

"Fifteen?"

"Maybe twenty," he admitted with a boyish grin.

Her laugh was sultry. "Points for honesty. So what did you think about for the first nineteen?"

The rough pad of a thumb scraped her bottom lip. "I thought about kissing you. Tasting you. Swallowing that smile. I figured somebody with a smile like that was somebody I needed to get to know. It brightens a room."

She swallowed hard, trying not to react too strongly to the gentleness of his words and tone. Innate sweetness had always been a part of Chaz's personality; it had been genuine, unfeigned. That kind, earnest streak was potent in combination with the hot masculinity he now possessed in spades.

Needing to return to sexy-and-edgy things and not sweetly-seductive things, she said, "And on the twentieth second?" Pursing her lips, she added, "What did you think then?"

"I plead the fifth."

"Chicken."

Not waiting for him to reply, she licked again while unfastening his belt and unbuttoning his jeans. Seeing that the tip of his erection was nudging out of the elastic at the top of his briefs, she moaned, deep in her throat. He had a lot to deposit, most definitely. More than she'd ever seen in her life, and for tonight, it was all hers.

Dying to taste him, she gently tugged the cotton down, revealing him to her hungry gaze, inch by inch. God, he was beautiful, bold, masculine and strong. She wanted him in every orifice of her body, starting with her mouth.

"Come on, admit it. You imagined this. Me on my knees, sucking you off," she said, still utterly fascinated by the awe-inspiring erection.

"Not on your knees." He sounded hoarse, needy.

She shifted her gaze to see him clenching both sides of the ATM. The tendons in his forearms flexed with the strain. He was dying for her mouth, she knew, but she drew things out, enjoying the sensual torment she was inflicting on them both.

"Where then?"

He scorched her with a glance, his eyes blazing with hunger. "I pictured you lying on top of me, turned around so you could suck my cock while I licked you into incoherence."

He didn't shock her, as he might have intended. "Sixty-nine is my favorite number."

"Mine, too."

"Maybe that's your pin number," she said with a saucy wink.

His response was more helpless groan than laugh. "Let's get out of here," he urged. "I'll take you to my place, get you in my bed and we'll talk about all our favorite numbers."

"First, I'd like to do some pleasuring. Now shut up."

He shut up.

Totally in the moment, uncaring of who might pull up outside, or what the camera above her head might record, she could focus only on the masculine perfection before her eyes. Lulu had worked the briefs down low enough to encircle as much of him as she could hold in one hand. Leaning closer, inhaling deeply to create another sense memory—one she would no doubt always associate with pure, driving need and hot, illicit sex—she flicked her tongue across the engorged tip, sampling his essence. His soft skin covered steel, and tasted salty and musky. Delicious.

Widening her mouth, she covered the tip of his erection and gently sucked, her tongue wetting him, her mouth devouring him. His hips instinctively thrust toward her, and she turned her head so he could go deeper. She took him in, sucking until that delicious cock filled her mouth, the end of him hitting the back of her throat, and then she greedily sucked a little bit more.

"Oh, yeah," he groaned, tangling both hands in her hair.

She ignored him, making oral love to him, taking him deep, then pulling away, tormenting him with every stroke. Chaz groaned mindlessly, and his hand tightened in her hair, coming close to the elastic that looped her mask over her ear.

Lulu instantly pulled away, missing the taste of him the moment that powerful shaft left her tongue.

"Huh-uh. You might be willing to risk showing your face, but I'm not," she said, hoping she sounded sexy and mysterious and not slightly desperate. Because, heaven help her, if he insisted that she take off the mask and reveal her true self to him, she wasn't sure she would be able to say no.

Maybe he wouldn't recognize you. Lust has clouded his brain; he might not have any idea who you are.

But she knew better than to think that might really happen. It might take a few seconds, and he wouldn't believe his eyes at first, but he would recognize her.

Besides, in the nearly impossible chance that he didn't, there was no way she could avoid seeing Chaz for the rest of her life, especially since she lived right down the street. He'd eventually find out who his mysterious witch had been.

"Sorry. I got carried away. I wouldn't expose you here."

Here. Right. But later? All bets would be off. It was madness to think that he wouldn't demand she take off the mask at his house. She had no idea why she'd believed she could get him to agree to anonymous, faceless sex. Which meant she might not be able to go through with her reckless plan to go home with the man and take whatever hot eroticisms he would be willing to offer a mysterious, unidentified woman.

Maybe he won't be that curious.

Yeah, and maybe a cop would pull up outside, smile, and tell them to carry on with what they were doing. Hell, the guy was a reporter. Chaz lived to solve riddles and get to the bottom of stories. He might let her blow him with a mask on her face for her own protection against the camera—typical, protective Chaz—but there was no way he'd let the mask stay there once they were assured of privacy.

Now might be all she had, unless she could figure out how to later reveal every bit of herself except her face.

"Am I forgiven?"

"Yes. But no unmasking, okay?"

"Cross my heart," he said, staring down at her, his hands braced on each side of the machine.

Sure of retaining her anonymity for a while longer, knowing she would probably never have another chance, Lulu concentrated on grabbing whatever illicit pleasure she could. She moved back to him, licking the shaft from base to tip.

"You taste so good, Chaz," she murmured as she shook off any unpleasant thoughts and focused only on the very pleasant task before her.

She reached down and cupped his tight balls, gently toying with them as she devoured his cock, concentrating as much on her own pleasure as on his. She loved how he tasted, loved all that heat and power in her mouth, loved knowing she was bringing him figuratively, if not literally, to his knees.

It didn't take long for him to reach that same state of mindlessness, and his groans signaled his impending release. Ever the gentleman, he cupped a hand around her cheek, trying to stop her. "Wait. No more."

She didn't let him push her away, determined to take him all the way. Gripping his hip, she kept sucking, and with just a few more pulls of her mouth, she got her reward. Shuddering, he came hard, his essence spurting against her tongue. She swallowed every warm, salty drop and licked her lips before releasing him and sagging back against the wall.

They both gasped for a while, and she watched him try to regain his composure. He'd been bracing himself against the machine, his eyes closed, so visibly delighted there could be no doubt something serious was happening out of view of the camera.

She wondered if anybody ever watched the security tapes without there being some kind of crime to investigate. Hopefully not. If they did, Chaz might have to find a new bank.

But right now, she suspected he wouldn't give a damn.

4

ALTHOUGH HE'D CLIMAXED so powerfully he'd thought the top of his head might blow off, Chaz was now even more desperate to get his mystery lover home. He quickly shoved himself back into his clothes, wondering how someone he'd just met could already be the most sexually addictive woman of his life.

She amazed him, thrilled him. Moments ago, she'd taken him to the ultimate heights, but just looking down at her, seeing the heave of her bare breasts as she tried to steady her breathing, he was already hard for her again.

She was stunning. Intriguing. So sexy. He'd never, in his entire life, been as driven by primal lust as he was tonight.

"Let's get out of here."

She busied herself fixing her bustier, not meeting his eye. "Maybe we could just stay here and…"

"Forget it," he bit out. "I want you totally naked and I don't want any interruptions or worries about privacy."

She hesitated, but he wasn't about to give her any time for doubts or regrets. All he could think about was tearing his pants open again, yanking those tights back down, and plunging balls deep into her tight pussy.

Bending down, he hauled her up, shifting them so his

back was to the camera, blocking any view of her. "I have to get you home. Now."

"Chaz, I…"

"I doubt we'll even make it past the foyer of my house," he told her. "There's a condom in my pocket and I'm tempted to put it on while we walk so I can fuck you the very second we close the front door."

She gazed at him, the mask still disguising far too much of her face. But the excitement in those eyes was unforgettable. "I like that idea."

Helping her up, he tightened the laces on her top and helped her refasten her black leather jacket. He could feel the thud of her heart as his knuckles brushed her chest. The woman was every bit as aroused as he was.

Leading her outside, he made good on his promise and picked her up, prepared to run home with her now that he knew she was in no way ready to call it a night.

She tried to protest. "This is silly, I can walk."

"Shut up. A deal's a deal."

"Are you always so stubborn?"

"I'm not at all stubborn. I'm the most easygoing guy around. Ask anybody."

"Then why don't you just agree to put me down before you break your back?"

"You're not exactly a wide load."

"I'm not exactly a featherweight, either."

He feigned insult. "You're offending my manliness."

Her responding laugh was cute and feminine. But he had to admit, she might have been right, because, as light as she was, after two blocks, his legs were complaining.

"Put me down, you big idiot. I fully intend to be fucked against your front door, and you won't be able to do that if you can't walk!"

He stopped, liking the way she thought, and really liking that she was so blunt about it. She seemed to be the kind of woman who went after what she wanted and made no apologies for it, which he found incredibly appealing. They might have danced around this a little bit at first, but now that the course was set, she wasn't steering off it.

"Okay, you win."

Pressing a kiss on her lips, he let her slide down his body, loving the instant when her parted legs hugged his hips and they came to within a few layers of fabric of ultimate connection. She ground against him, and he thrust back, his cock painfully hard and desperately in need of hot, wet woman.

Needing another taste before they completed the walk home, he carried her over to the nearest tree and leaned her against it. Bending his face to hers, he kissed her hungrily, exploring the soft, wonderful places in her mouth. Their bodies ground together, mimicking the heated act they'd be completing if not for their clothing.

"I want in," he groaned.

"And I want you in," she whimpered. "Stupid tights."

"They're awesome tights. But right now I'd like to rip them with my teeth."

She hissed into his mouth, bucking a little as she envisioned it. "Why don't you just use your hands instead?"

He stared down at her, wondering what she meant, then getting it. He couldn't decide at first if she was serious. They were not in a brightly lit vestibule anymore, they were half hidden in the shadows of a tree. But still….

"Right here? Right now?"

"Yes," she begged, arching harder against him. "Just a taste, Chaz. Give me something to tide me over for another few blocks."

He reached between her heated thighs, felt the dampness of her crotch and dug his fingers into the weave of the tights, easily pulling them apart. Sighing with relief, with masculine satisfaction, he fingered her, finding her every bit as wet as she'd been before.

Letting most of her weight rest against the tree, he quickly unfastened his pants. His cock sprang hot and hard into his hand. It brushed against her thigh, and she moaned and tightened her legs around him, pulling him close to her heat.

"Please, Chaz," she begged, writhing, thrusting her hips forward to take what he wasn't yet giving her.

It was insane. They were outside on a public street, in one of the biggest cities in the country. But there was something dark and elemental about the night. Maybe it was the late hour. Maybe it was because of the date on the calendar—Halloween night. Maybe it was the bright moon or the long, narrow clouds drifting across the inky sky or the sense of surreal, all-encompassing attraction he'd felt from the moment he'd laid eyes on her. Something just wouldn't let him stop without grabbing this hedonistic, dangerous moment of sin.

He began to slip into her, his cock inching in, gobbled by her silky, wet flesh. From the very first moment of possession, he was shaken by the primitive desire to pour himself into her. He wanted to make a permanent place for himself inside her body, to bury himself so deeply she would never remember what it felt like before he'd taken her.

He'd pushed no more than an inch, barely even the head of his dick, into her, getting nothing but a taste of her sweet tightness, when a car came by, slowing and beeping as someone cat-called out the window.

"Fuck," he groaned, immediately pulling away, lowering her to stand, and tugging her skirt down into place. He quickly spun around, his back toward the street, blocking her from view, and trying to fix jeans that were suddenly way too tight.

"Oh, God, just shoot me now," she groaned.

He glared over his shoulder at the occupants of the offending vehicle, hidden within shadows behind closed windows. The car quickly sped up and tore off down the street with another honk of the horn and a squeal of tires.

"They're gone."

"Did you get that tag number? I'm going to put a hit out on them," she said, sounding tortured by sensual need.

Although it physically pained him, he managed to get his clothes around his steel-hard cock, shoving it behind his seam as he heaved in deep breaths of cold night air.

"It's not much farther to my house," he said, swallowing in an attempt to calm himself down. His heart was racing, his blood coursing hotly through his veins. If he closed his eyes, he could almost feel her still, and it was easy to imagine what it would be like to sink all the way into her and be wrapped in all that silky warmth. "Can you run in those damn shoes?"

"I'll crawl if I have to," she said, her vehemence both cute and flattering. "And FYI, if you'd like to revisit that particular position as soon as we're behind closed doors, I definitely won't complain," she said sounding breathless.

"You've got a deal."

Both anticipating that moment now more than ever, they returned to the sidewalk, walking together, hip-to-hip, thigh brushing thigh. He slid an arm around her waist, tugging her close, and she pressed her cheek against his shoulder, her head fitting there just perfectly. They didn't run, but there was purpose in their strides, a hunger for what would come when they reached their destination.

A chime suddenly interrupted the quiet night. "Crap, let

me turn this off." She glanced into her purse and retrieved her phone, quickly scanning the message on the screen.

"Problem?"

Sighing, she asked, "Are you going to rape me, then murder me and make a lampshade out of my skin?"

He almost tripped over his own feet, coming to a stop and spinning to face her. "Excuse me?"

"My friend Viv, from back at the bar. She finally stopped dirty-dancing with an entire football team and realized I was gone. Now she's harassing me for leaving with you, as if you're Hannibal Lecter's long-lost twin."

"Please assure her that I'm not a rapist, or a killer, or an interior decorator."

It took her less than a second, then her lips twitched. "Ha. Very funny. So I can assure her my skin is going to stay where it is?"

"It seems to be doing a very good job in its present location," he said, casting an appreciative eye over her, from windswept red hair down to her wickedly sexy shoes.

In fact, he wouldn't change a single thing about her. Except for removing that mask. Oh, and the rest of her clothes.

"Thank you," she said, her voice so proper and prim and adorable, he had to tug her close for another quick brush of lips on lips.

Realizing her friend was just being protective, and that she had the right to be, considering this relationship was moving super-fast and had so far involved acts that would probably get them arrested for indecency, he said, "Tell her I'm going to make wild love to you all night, then get up and make you waffles for breakfast."

That sounded like the perfect way to spend his first night and following morning home.

She lowered her eyes and stepped away from him. "Um…"

"You don't like waffles? All right, pancakes it is."

"Listen, the first half of that sounds wonderful." She twisted her hands in front of her, her eyes on her own fingers. "But I'm not looking for anything serious here."

"If I were making Peking duck, I might consider that serious, but we're talking breakfast food here. How about Lucky Charms? How serious can a cereal with marshmallows in it be?"

"They're my favorite," she admitted with a sheepish sigh.

"Mine, too. I once broke up with a woman who told me she wouldn't allow a kids' cereal at her breakfast table."

"Guess she didn't want kids."

"We hadn't really reached that stage yet. But on behalf of any potential future children she might have, I called her bluff and didn't see her again."

"Dumped over a box of cereal. Harsh."

"Hey, don't mess with a man's one weakness."

"I'll remember that."

"Tomorrow morning?"

She immediately realized she'd backed herself into a corner. "Uh, wait, no, that's not what I meant." She tucked a strand of wildly blowing hair behind her ear, visibly stalling. Taking a deep breath, she admitted, "Breakfast implies an all-nighter."

"You doubting my manhood again?" he asked, deliberately misunderstanding her. He knew she was skittish and was backing away from the idea of actually spending an entire night in his bed. Hell, if she thought up-against-the-front-door sex was all he was after, she didn't rate her own appeal very highly. After what they'd already shared, what she'd already made him feel, he wasn't sure he'd be willing to let her out of his sight for a month.

"Not at all," she said, her smile tremulous. "It's just, I'm not thinking long-term here."

"And tomorrow morning is oh-so-far away?"

"Too far away for my taste."

Huh. She'd really surprised him. He hadn't had many one-night-stands, but he felt pretty sure that women got testy if they thought you didn't want them to actually sleep with you once they'd been invited to, uh, *sleep* with you.

"I like you," he admitted with a shrug. "Going to bed with you tonight and waking up with you tomorrow won't exactly be a hardship."

"It might if you knew who you'd be waking up with."

"You mean, the wicked witch?"

"Something like that."

"I'm a big boy. I'll take my chances."

She swallowed, her throat quivering. A gusty wind howled through the night, and she pulled her coat tighter around herself. Chaz stepped closer to block the wind, enjoying the way her hair blew against his face. Not to mention how deliciously soft her skin felt against the tips of his fingers. The memory of sinking just one inch inside that beautiful body made him shake with need, from head to toe.

Yeah. He would definitely take his chances. He'd savor whatever she wanted to give him and then figure out how to make her want to give him more.

He reached for her chin and lifted it, forcing her to look at him. The silly mask remained on her face, and he couldn't wait to take it off. But he sensed they were doing that dance again, like they'd done in the bar. *Forward and back.* He didn't want to do anything to push her away.

"Just come home with me," he urged, "and let the chips fall where they may."

She stared up at him, uncertainty awash in those shaded eyes. "With no promises?"

He sensed she needed an out. Hoping she'd change her mind, he nodded. "No promises." Lightening the mood, he grinned. "And no lampshades."

She visibly relaxed, her stiff posture loosening, her tight mouth softening. "That's a deal."

"Are you going to let your friend know?"

She glanced at her phone, tapped out a brief message, and then turned the device off. "I'm all yours," she said once she'd dropped it back into her purse. "For the next hour or so, anyway."

"There you go, doubting my manliness again."

"Three hours?"

"At a bare minimum."

However long it lasted, he would never forget it. Nothing like this had ever happened to him before, and he was already sure that he was in the middle of something very special. Possibly life-changing. He couldn't say how he knew it—maybe intuition, maybe wishful thinking. It didn't matter. He was just certain, on some elemental level, that he would be irrevocably changed after this night.

They started walking again, but hadn't gone more than a couple of feet before he heard her soft giggle. So maybe she wasn't thinking about anything on an elemental level.

Which was just one more thing he liked about her. She was damned unpredictable.

"What now?"

"I just had this mental image of somebody at that savings and loan watching the video and wondering what in hell was going on when you stood there for so long with your head thrown back."

He thrust a hand through his hair, wondering where on earth the two of them had gotten the nerve to be so outrageous. He could practically see the headlines now: *Local Reporter Charged With Indecency In A Bank Lobby.* Wouldn't his friends and colleagues have a field day with that one?

Still, he couldn't bring himself to regret it. "I suppose that depends on who was watching."

"You might want to change where you do your banking."

He wasn't worried. "I really don't think they watch those recordings unless they have a reason to review them for a crime or something."

"Then let's hope nobody robs the place tonight. I'm so not ready for my *close-up* to be seen by an audience."

"Your *close-up* was my favorite part of the whole banking experience," he admitted, unable to deny it. "But even if somebody does watch, that camera didn't capture anything below waist level."

And if it had, there'd be nothing to see except a mass of glorious, curly red hair.

Christ, the thought of what she'd done to him—how she'd made him feel—was enough to make him want to throw his head back and howl to the moon like a werewolf on the prowl this Halloween night. Her sexual generosity had stunned him.

"You know, I've dated women for months who didn't do for me what you did back there."

"Do you mean going with you to the ATM so you could, uh—" she licked her lips "—make a *deposit?*"

God, she was outrageous. "Yeah. You didn't have to actually let me complete my…deposit."

"I enjoyed it." She shrugged, sounding as though she meant it.

"I thought women only enjoyed it on a guy's birthday or after getting a diamond bracelet or something."

"You calling me cheap for settling for a cherry-flavored drink and a dance?"

"There is nothing cheap about you," he insisted with a squeeze of her hand. "Absolutely nothing."

"I'm kidding. But there was no quid pro quo about it," she said. "I wanted to taste you."

"You didn't have to go for the full-course meal and swallow every morsel."

She stopped and turned on her heel to look up at him. "I told you before, I'm not a cock-tease. I wasn't going to bring you up the mountain and not let you jump off the highest cliff." She lifted up on her tiptoes and brushed her lips against his. "You taste good."

He tugged her close and covered her mouth for a kiss, sweeping his tongue inside to explore her all over again. She twined around his body like a vine around a post, pressing every inch of herself against him. By the time the kiss ended, he was barely able to catch his breath. His heart thudded, his pants refused to stay zipped to the top, and he found himself wishing he hadn't insisted they leave the vestibule. And cursing that stupid honking car to the ninth circle of hell.

Letting her go, he said, "Come on, we're almost there."

She nodded, twined her fingers in his and matched him stride for stride as they headed down the street. They passed one young couple, dressed as a pair of comic book superheroes, who barely managed to stop groping each other as they walked by. He wondered if he and his mystery woman had just interrupted the couple the same way the car had interrupted them. The other couple hadn't seemed to rush to put any clothes back in place, but he would bet they weren't more than a few minutes from reaching that point.

"Happy Halloween," he said with a grin as they passed.

"You, too," the guy said. "Hope you get lots of treats."

Chaz fully intended to.

"That's my place on the corner," he said, nodding toward his townhouse.

"Good thing, these shoes are killing me," she said.

"Serves you right for doubting my manhood."

"I didn't doubt your manhood. Just your wisdom."

That startled another laugh out of him. Damn, how he liked this woman.

"Well, I don't see any toilet paper or eggshells, so I guess the trick-or-treaters didn't punish you for not being home to give out any candy."

"A few knocked before I went to the bar. I handed out a couple of bags of airplane crackers and some Altoids."

"They should've egged your house just for that."

She was probably right. Fortunately, no angry, deprived-of-candy ghosts or goblins had played tricks after he'd left.

Yanking her hand from his, she suddenly stopped. "Who's that?"

"Huh?"

"The woman sitting on the car over there."

Realizing she was looking toward one of the reserved parking spaces directly in front of his house, he followed her stare. A bright yellow Beetle was parked beside his own car, and on the hood of it sat a woman. She was draped in gauzy white fabric that might have been a toga or might have been a ghost-sheet like the one he'd worn.

Chaz scrunched his brow for a moment, wondering why some stranger was sitting alone on the hood of her car at this time of night. Then he spotted the hair, as yellow as the vehicle, and realized who it was.

"Shit." He turned to his mystery witch. "It's my sister."

"Sarah," she whispered.

Taken aback for a moment, he suddenly remembered he had mentioned his sibling's name at the club. "Yes. I have no idea what she's doing here."

"She looks upset." There was a hint of coldness in the tone that hadn't been there all evening. It appeared he wasn't the only one disappointed that someone had delayed them from getting inside for their promised up-against-the-wall adventure. His sister had the worst timing in the universe. Well, second worse. That car honking was number one.

"There you are," Sarah said, sliding off the car and sniffing audibly. *Definitely a toga. Roman goddess?* "Mom said you got back to town today and I just had to see you and you weren't *he-re* when I *neeeeded* you! Where have you *be-en?*"

"Have any cheese you can give her to go with that whine?" his companion muttered.

Chaz smothered a laugh, because, yes, Sarah had sounded like a whiny brat. Which wasn't exactly an uncommon occurrence. She was the baby of the family and relished the role, getting her way in just about everything she'd ever wanted.

"Don't move," he said, reluctantly dropping his companion's hand. "I'll find out what's going on and be right back."

He strode toward his pain in the ass of a sister. "Hey, kid, what's up?"

"I've been waiting for you, big brother. I feel like I'm going crazy!" Sarah threw her arms around his neck, bur-

ied her face in his chest and began sobbing loudly. "I'm
so miserable!"

So much for *Welcome home. How's it going? I've missed
you.*

He returned the hug, smoothing her hair, wondering
what on earth the big drama was this time.

"I can't believe you didn't let me know you were home
and ask me if I wanted to do something tonight," she said.

"I figured you had plans with your friends."

"I did. I mean, I do."

"So what's the problem?"

"Everything fell apart."

Maybe for her. But things had fallen into *place* for him,
and he didn't want anything to change that. "I intended to
call you tomorrow. Now what's wrong?"

"You will not believe who I ran into today."

"The president?"

She pulled away and scowled at him. "No! Can you believe Lawrence Vandenberg is going to A.U. for his master's degree and he lives right beside the campus and Mom
never warned me?"

Oh. That. "I heard. Lulu mentioned it in an email."

Sarah's jaw dropped. "You keep in touch with *her?*
After what her stupid brother did to me?"

"Not regularly, that's for sure. She moved here. Mom
gave her my email address so she could get some information on housing and stuff."

That was the full extent of his contact with the girl-
next-door, and he wanted to keep it that way. Lulu Vandenberg had been the most annoying next-door neighbor
any geeky kid should have to endure, and he was lucky
he'd made it out of his childhood with his sanity—and his
tailbone—intact.

He did vaguely wonder how she'd turned out. Lulu had,

after all, been one of the prettiest girls he'd ever known, not that he would never have told her he thought so in a million years. Maybe she'd grown up to be a hag, though he doubted it. Her emails had been friendly and chatty, brimming with self-confidence. Of course, Lulu had been that way, too. Always talking, always ready to hand out advice. She'd been a real know-it-all.

Nah. He didn't really want to see how she'd turned out.

"She had the nerve to ask you for help after the way she always treated you when we were kids?" Sarah said, finally thinking of someone other than herself.

To be fair, Lulu hadn't been *all* bad. They'd actually gotten along fine much of the time, usually by ignoring each other. It was just that she was so damned bossy, and good at everything. She'd out-played him on the basketball court, had ridden her bike in circles around him while he still struggled with his first ten-speed. She was the bravest and the toughest when it came to playing truth-or-dare. She was also dangerous—he'd been a witness to the great playground fight, when she, at age eight, had slugged an eleven-year-old boy who made fun of six-year-old Lawrence for still having a teddy bear.

And of course there was the ladder incident. Sometimes, when he sat down just the right way, he still got a twinge out of that forever-cracked tailbone.

"It's no big deal. Mom asked me to help out. Lulu's her best friend's kid. What was I supposed to do, say no?"

"Well, hopefully you told her the safest place in the city to live is Anacostia," Sarah said with a heaping helping of spite, since that neighborhood was one of the most dangerous in the district.

Chaz grunted. "Let it go, little sister."

It was kid stuff, and he'd tried to forget it. That said,

he did hope his Realtor had found Lulu an apartment far away from his own neighborhood.

"What, exactly, did Lulu tell you about Lawrence?" she asked.

"Just that he was coming here to go to school, too."

"Did she mention that he was doing it so he could be close to some girl?"

Chaz stayed quiet, sensing a trap in the question.

Eventually Sarah continued. "Because he happens to have a girlfriend! And I think they might be living together!"

From several feet away, where he'd left his sexy witch, he heard a cough, but he stayed focused on Sarah, knowing he had to hear her out, give her a brotherly word of wisdom, and then send her on her way. "And that's your business…why?"

She sputtered. "Well, he had to have been aware I'm at A.U. He did it on purpose, came here just to get close to me and try to make me jealous."

"Is it working?"

"No, it is not. That's ridiculous."

"Great. Then there's no problem."

She gritted her teeth and literally growled at him. "Of course there's a problem."

He had never found out exactly what had happened between his sister and Lawrence. Nor was he sure he wanted to. Knowing his sister, and well aware that Lawrence was a great guy, he had to assume Sarah had been at fault, not that he was about to say that to her. He valued his eardrums too much; she would scream the neighborhood down if he accused her of being anything but the injured party in that long-ago breakup. The key being *long ago.*

"Sarah, it's been years. Why haven't you moved on?"

Her bottom lip pushed out and her big blue eyes grew

moist. He could see unshed tears, illuminated by the street light overhead. Damn it, his sister really could turn on the waterworks.

"You just don't understand." Sniff. "Of course you'd take his side. You're such a guy."

"I understand breakups and exes. I've had my share."

He didn't add that he was the one who usually did the breaking up, his job being a lot more important to him than anyone he'd ever dated. And most women his age didn't want to wait around for weeks at a time while he jet-setted his way across the globe chasing stories.

There had been one who'd seemed like she could handle it. She'd assured him she could, in fact. Then he'd come home early from a trip and gone to surprise her at her place.

Surprise! She was dating another dude on the side, and had been for a while.

They hadn't had any exclusive agreement or anything, but she'd told him flat-out that she wasn't seeing anyone else. He could take a woman who dated others, but he would not put up with one who lied. In his line of work, where he had to rely on sources, he had absolutely zero tolerance for liars. He'd devoted most of his efforts to tyrants and warlords, but even the lowliest liar could do serious damage. He'd seen friends' careers ruined because of other people's falsehoods, which was bad enough. Worse were the deceptions that put others in harm's way. In some of the darker, more dangerous countries he had visited, deliberate lies had lured journalists to their own brutal deaths, and Chaz was always slow to give his trust and quick to take it back if it were betrayed.

"Listen, why don't you go ahead with your plans for tonight. Go have fun, you'll feel better. I'll take you out for breakfast on Sunday." Seeing that she was considering it, he added the key point. "I'll bet running into you didn't make Lawrence change his plans."

That did it. The crocodile tears dried immediately and her shoulders squared. "You're right. I can't give him the satisfaction of knowing he ruined my Halloween."

"Atta girl," he said, squeezing her arm and gently pushing her toward her car. He opened the door and helped her shove all the loose fabric of her costume inside.

She rolled down the window and blew him a kiss. "Thanks, Chaz. Happy Halloween. Have fun with your... oh, where'd she go?"

"Who?"

"Weren't you with someone?" she asked, craning to look through the windshield at the sidewalk.

The empty sidewalk.

He didn't panic. "She must have gone up to the porch to wait for me."

Sarah sat up higher in her seat and peered toward the front of his house. "Nope, nobody there."

"I'm sure she's around," he said, not worrying...not really, anyway. "Call me tomorrow about breakfast."

Sarah agreed and then backed up the car and drove away. The second she was out of sight, Chaz spun around to return to his companion. He assumed he'd find her in the shadows of one of the large live oak trees that lined the front of the row of townhouses. But she wasn't there.

His heart rate kicked up. He strode toward his own place, searching the porch and the walkway, then retraced his steps.

"Are we playing hide-and-seek now?" he asked out loud, feeling stupid for not having gotten her name. He didn't particularly want to call out, "Hey, sexy witch who just gave me the best blow job of my life, where are you?"

Dry leaves scuttled along the sidewalk and a strong

breeze howled up the empty street, whistling between the cars. There was no other sound. No response.

No beautiful woman.

Not believing his own senses, he looked again, retracing their steps, checking behind each car, going all the way up to the corner. By the time he reached the bank vestibule and saw it empty, something akin to panic made him break into a sweat until he was almost running to the bar. But somehow, he knew even before he went inside and scanned the entire place, table by table, that he wasn't going to find her.

Every minute, every step, every peering glance reinforced in his heart what his head had already begun to accept.

She was gone. His mystery woman, the one he'd been sure was going to become his utter sexual obsession, had disappeared.

5

Lulu woke up the day after Halloween to a dull headache, but she didn't attribute it to the devilish red drinks she'd consumed at the bar. Oh, no. The ache behind her eyes and the throbbing in her temple had been caused by the long hours she'd lain awake, kicking herself for two things: first, leaving with Chaz and indulging in that wickedly erotic encounter at the bank; and second, running out on him right before they went into his house to have the kind of wild sex she knew would have lived in her memories forever.

Her brain was more regretful about the first, her body the second.

"You are so stupid," she reminded herself as she rolled out of bed and eyed her wild, red-tinted hair in the mirror over her dresser. "Not to mention a damn coward."

She'd been all set to risk it, to take a chance and hope Chaz wouldn't recognize her after they had the kind of sex that was probably illegal in some states.

Then his spoiled kid sister had shown up—to complain about Lulu's sweetheart of a kid brother. It had taken a lot of willpower to stay quiet when Sarah had made the comment about Lawrence living with a girlfriend, which was news to Lulu. She'd gasped so loud she'd had to turn the sound into a cough to cover the reaction.

Plus, not only had Sarah brought reality crashing down on Lulu like a ton of cement, but she'd also upped the risk factor. If Lulu hadn't gotten out of there, it was very possible Chaz would have invited her over to meet his sister. And while Chaz hadn't seen or heard her in years, Sarah definitely had. They had spoken last summer when they'd both been visiting their respective parents. If Sarah didn't figure out who owned the face behind the mask just on sight—by the shape of her mouth or the darkness of her eyes—she would almost certainly recognize Lulu's voice.

Overhearing part of their conversation had added fuel to the fire beneath her feet for another reason, as well. There was just too much baggage between her and Chaz. It hadn't been easy hearing Sarah remind her brother of how much he disliked Lulu, and ask why he'd ever agreed to help her with anything.

Did Chaz really hate her? His sister had made it sound as if he had reason to. Oh, yes, she'd been a little shit to him on occasion, but she'd never been vicious or deliberately cruel. God, she hated to think he might be carrying scars even deeper than the ones she'd taken for granted.

The very idea had made the whole escapade seem tawdry and unkind. She had no business tricking a night of sensuality out of a guy who hated her guts. Going home with him like that was akin to stealing. He had every right to know who she was and shoot her down, and she'd taken away his chance.

So she'd played the coward and darted away while Chaz and Sarah had been talking. She'd slipped around the side of the townhouse row, heading for her own building down the block and entering the back door. Watching through her window as he'd gone looking for her, she had bitten her lip and let tears fall from her eyes as she recognized his frustration.

"Frustration is better than fury."

Right. And Chaz *would* be furious if he found out who she really was. Meaning she had to be more careful than ever not to give him any clue that she was the woman who'd been on her knees giving him the blow job to end all blow jobs last night.

Although she loved her cute apartment, and her neighbors, and the area, she suddenly found herself wishing she'd found a place in another part of the city. Now that he was home, chances were good she would run into Chaz sometime soon. She only hoped she was ready to come face to face with him again, without revealing everything she was thinking.

Trying to put the memories of the night before out of her mind, she went to take a long, hot shower. The spray-in hair color was temporary, but she still had to wash her hair three times before she felt confident the glittery stuff was completely gone. And after she got out of the shower, brushed her hair, and spotted a few incriminating auburn streaks, she went right back in and washed it again.

Finally, when she'd made sure to remove every wisp of color and had thrust her witch costume into the darkest corner of her closet, she pulled on jeans and a sweater, wanting to get out of her apartment. It was a beautiful fall day—sunny, breezy, the sky clear and Robin's egg–blue—and she was determined to stop hiding inside and go out to enjoy the weather. Winter wouldn't be far away now, and while it would never be as bad as the winters in the mountains of western Maryland, where she'd grown up, she knew she'd soon be missing these sunny, cool days.

Heading out her door and down the stairs, she bumped into the couple who lived in the apartment directly above hers. She hadn't known them long, but she already liked them a lot, appreciating the way the women had immediately been neighborly without being intrusive.

"Hey, Lulu," said Marcia, who was carrying a bag of groceries in one hand and was shoving her glasses up her nose with the other.

"Morning," she replied, holding the front door of the building open so Marcia and Peggy could come inside with their groceries.

"Did you have a good Halloween?" asked Peggy.

"It was…interesting," she admitted.

That was an understatement.

"It must have been if you slept so heavily this morning that you didn't notice all the commotion around here," Marcia said, her voice filled with amusement.

"Why? What happened?"

"Peggy played hero for some kid whose kitty got stuck in the tree out front. She climbed up to rescue it."

Lulu's eyes widened in surprise. The tree was a monster; she'd seen last spring's kites still tangled in its branches. "You didn't go too high, did you?"

Peggy groaned, embarrassed.

"Yes, she did," said Marcia, dropping an arm across the other woman's shoulders. "She made the mistake of looking down."

"I never knew I was afraid of heights," Peggy said, gazing at her feet and scuffing her toe on the tiled floor.

"I had to call 911 and a fire crew came and helped her down."

"Damn, I missed hot firefighters?"

"Well, there was one hot one," said Peggy, "but I don't think she was your type."

"She wasn't yours, either," said Marcia with a smirk as she held up her left hand, on which glittered a gold wedding band. The two had gotten married this past summer, happy to be in a city that celebrated freedom and let them live their lives exactly as they wanted to.

"And I wouldn't have it any other way," said Peggy, lightly kissing her wife's cheek. Turning to Lulu, she asked, "Where you off to?"

"Just out for a walk. It's too nice to stay inside."

"Definitely. Tomorrow's supposed to be even nicer. Why don't you join us out back for dinner then? We're going to have one final grill-out of the fall. The couple from the first floor is coming. It'll be a BYOM party."

"BYOM?"

"Bring your own meat."

Promising she would join them the next day, Lulu said goodbye to the couple and headed outside. She turned right at the sidewalk, as usual. Then she hesitated. Chaz's house was so close, she'd have to walk right past it. He might be sleeping off his travel jet lag. Or he might be sleeping because he'd been up all night wondering about the woman who'd run out on him. Or he might be wide awake, plotting his revenge.

Hell. It was worth taking a different route today.

She spun around, ready to do exactly that, when a male voice called out, "Hey, you! Wait a minute—stop!"

There was no denying that voice, or the demanding tone. It was Chaz.

Closing her eyes and taking a deep breath, she turned around to face the music. There was no point delaying the inevitable. She'd have to see him sometime and part of her just wanted to get it over with and stop worrying about it.

Another part was wondering how, exactly, she would react if he recognized her not as his childhood nemesis, but as his almost-lover of the previous night. He'd seen her from behind, but had called out with something that sounded like desperation. So she suspected he'd been searching for his mystery woman, and believed he'd spotted her.

Now the question remained: was this morning's encounter going to end in anger, ambivalence or attempted seduction?

Chaz was jogging up the sidewalk, looking determined, but he slowed to a walk when he got a good look at her. A confused frown tugged at his brow as he studied her, his gaze resting on her long brown hair, then traveling over her face. She knew the exact moment he recognized her, because his mouth opened in a quick, surprised inhalation, and his eyes widened in shock.

"Lulu? Is that you?"

She pasted a smile on her lips. "It sure is. Hi, Chaz!" She cursed herself for sounding giddy—and guilty. "Er, how are you doing? I guess you're home from your trip?" She made sure to keep her voice pitched up a bit, wanting to sound as far from the throaty-voiced temptress of the night as possible.

His long-legged strides brought him to within a few feet of her, and he stopped, staring into her face as if searching for something. Or someone?

Don't find her. Please don't find her in me.

"It's really you?" he asked.

"Yup." She forced the brightest, most unconcerned smile she could manage. "I guess I turned up just like the proverbial bad penny."

"This is a surprise."

More like a shock, judging by his expression.

"A nice one, I hope," she said, just to needle him a little.

"Sure. Definitely."

Deciding to remind him it had been partially his fault that they'd ended up neighbors, she said, "Oh, thanks bunches for putting me in touch with your Realtor. She was such a big help. She told me this was the best street in the city to live on."

She waved toward the building she'd just left, and Chaz glanced at it, then back at her.

"You live here?"

"Yes."

"Right here," he clarified, tensing. "Three doors down from me?"

"'Fraid so."

He continued to stare, and she shifted uncomfortably on her sneakered feet. She hadn't expected Chaz to bring out the welcome wagon, but yeesh, he acted as if she'd contaminated his street.

Finally she asked, "Do I have dirt on my face or something?"

"I'm sorry," he mumbled. "When I first saw you, from behind, I thought you were somebody else. But of course, I was wrong."

"They say everybody has a double."

He slowly shook his head, and she'd swear disappointment had darkened his eyes. "No, it was just a mistake. She didn't really look like you at all."

Huh. What was that supposed to mean? She felt as if she'd been judged and found lacking. What, exactly, did the green-faced witch have that she didn't, aside from red hair and a mask?

Oh. Right. An untainted history and a name other than Lulu Vandenberg. Even if she were a real redhead, and still had on the dumb mask, she suspected that Chaz would have worn that same expression of disappointment the moment he realized who she truly was.

Shoving aside the sharp feeling of regret, she tried to appear chipper. "So, how's your family?"

"They seem fine. I talked to my dad this morning." He

chuckled. "Did you hear? We're all being abandoned for Thanksgiving."

Her jaw dropped. "What?"

"Yeah. My family usually meets up at my grandparents' house down in Virginia for the holiday weekend."

"I remember." That was one reason she hadn't seen Chaz in so many years. He never came home for Thanksgiving, as his family was always traveling elsewhere. And it seemed the two of them had alternated Christmases for the past several years, never making a holiday trip home at the same time.

"Well, apparently our parents—yours and mine—have decided to go on a couples cruise to the Caribbean over Thanksgiving weekend. They're leaving the Tuesday before and will be gone for ten days."

"Nice of them to tell a person," she said, indignant. Then mischief tickled her lips and she grinned. "You'd think they had a life other than us, or something."

"I know, right?" he replied, sounding just as indignant-yet-amused.

Just to rile him up, she smirked. "I bet yours have already turned your room into a sex den like out of that *Fifty Shades* book."

He grimaced. "I know you opened your mouth and said something, but all I heard was mwah mwah mwah mwah mwah."

She couldn't hold back a rumble of laughter. When they were kids, they'd all mimicked their parents—well, all adults—in just that way. Words might be coming out of a grown-up's mouth, but all they'd heard was monotonous noise—like all kids, she supposed.

Funny how the adult world existed so far apart from the kid one, neither believing the other was ever really aware of what was going on. Also funny that she was standing here with a man who'd shared so many years of that world with her.

Yet gazing up at him, she saw nothing of the kid and every inch of the man.

What a delicious-looking man. He was sexy by moonlight, but devastatingly attractive in the light of day. The sun gleamed in his blond hair, and brought out the matching glimmer of gold in his green eyes. Now, clad in sneakers instead of those deadly high-heels, she was reminded just how tall he was, towering over her by several inches. And the long-sleeved T-shirt emphasized those broad shoulders and his powerful chest.

She'd have liked to say that quip about the naughty book hadn't caused some seriously hawt images to invade her brain, but she'd have been lying. Frankly, she'd had those images in her head since she'd seen him pulling off that sheet last night at the bar, and just about every minute since.

"So," he said, "I guess that means I'm going to have to learn how to cook a turkey."

"I hear Stauffer's does a pretty good job of that, and you get the stuffing and gravy right on top of it."

He sneered. "Frozen dinners for Thanksgiving? Forget it. How tough can it be?"

"Just remember to take the insides out of the bird before you cook it."

He paled. "They come with insides?"

"Pretty gross, huh?" Lulu had never been much of a cook, but she was pretty sure they did. "But yeah, I think so. And don't worry, I'll play dumb when my mom calls. I won't let her know you spilled the beans."

"Admit it, you just want to torment her and make her feel guilty."

"Ha. I think I'll call *her* and tell her I'm bringing home my new boyfriend for the holiday."

His smile remained, though she would swear it was a tiny bit tighter than before. She quickly thrust the impression away. Ridiculous to think Chaz would give a damn if she was dating anyone.

"You're seeing someone?"

Okay. So he gave a damn. Interesting.

She thought about implying she was but honestly didn't want to play those kinds of games with Chaz. Last night was as much gaming as she cared to do with the man. Besides, intentionally making somebody jealous was more his sister's style. "No. But I can't come up with a better way to make her sweat."

"You're an evil woman, Lulu Vandenberg," he said, the tone admiring.

"Diabolical, that's me. How could you have forgotten?"

"I haven't. But evil looks a little better on you than it did when you were seven and you tied me up to a telephone pole during a game of cops and robbers, and *left* me there."

Yeah. She'd kind of done that. "If it's any consolation, my mom spanked me after your parents called the police to report you missing and I had to tell the officers where you were."

"You deserved it."

"I guess I did. I'm really surprised you didn't just clobber me."

"I thought about it every day of our childhood." Amusement danced in his green eyes. "But maybe I just always wanted to believe my mom was right."

"About?"

"She used to say you tormented me so much because you secretly had a crush on me."

Lulu's mouth opened and then snapped closed. He

sounded so amused, so damned confident, as if he'd decided his mom was right.

"In your dreams, Chaz Browning."

"You were. Often."

Her brow shot up. So did her heart rate.

"Well, in my nightmares, anyway."

She couldn't help it. She balled her fist and punched his upper arm.

He rubbed at it, giving an exaggerated groan, then broke into a smile. "You still hit like a girl."

"Do you?"

"Uh-uh."

No, she didn't imagine he did, not with those muscle-bearing-muscles.

"I thought you were a lover, not a fighter."

He certainly had seemed that way last night, when he'd been so close, so very close, to becoming her lover. Damn it, why had Sarah shown up and scared her into running away from what she suspected would have been one of the best nights of her life?

"I am. But I sometimes go to some pretty dangerous places. I took up martial arts, just to be on the safe side."

Lulu didn't like to think of him needing to defend himself, though she knew he'd probably had to at one time or another. But it was a reminder of all the reasons why they could never work.

"Did anything like that happen on your most recent trip?" she asked.

"Nah. Totally uneventful. It was pretty boring."

Right. Except for his quick little excursions into freaking Afghanistan. Not that she could tell him she knew about that.

It had been easier when they'd been strangers.

"When did you get back?" she asked, since it seemed to be the sort of question she should ask.

"Yesterday. Just in time to go out and celebrate the holiday." He shook his head, as if clearing it of confusing memories, then managed a friendly, if noncommittal, smile. "It was a pretty long trip."

"You go away a lot?"

"Yes. My job is everything to me, but it has its downsides."

"Like?"

"Like…well, I can't have a dog. I'm away too much."

"I imagine that would be next to impossible."

"Ah, well, I guess I'm a one-dog man, anyway."

She understood, remembering how much Chaz had always adored his beagle.

"I do keep him close, though," he said.

Raising a curious brow, she watched as he pulled his shirt collar down a little, and tugged it away from his skin, just enough for her to make out the ink on his back. Finally, she was able to see what she hadn't been able to make out last night: his tattoo. The image of a cute little dog was etched on his shoulder, a constant reminder and a tribute to a beloved pet.

How very Chaz-like.

Part of her melted, wanting to hug him to commiserate, and wanting to ask him how somebody so utterly gorgeous and so incredibly nice could possibly still be single.

Another part reminded her she needed to keep up as many barriers as she could, if only to prevent him from ever finding out how she'd tricked him the night before. Chaz had always been very forgiving, but she remembered he'd had a real problem with liars—something he'd said had only intensified with the high stakes of his job. While she didn't think she'd actually said anything that was a lie, she was certainly guilty of it by omission.

One thing she knew, however. It was going to be very difficult to keep her secret about how attracted she was to him if he kept doing things like pulling his shirt down to reveal his powerful, muscular shoulders and back.

Damn you, Sarah, for making me realize I was making a mistake about twenty minutes too soon!

"Anyway, enough about me. How are you enjoying the city so far?"

"I love it," she admitted. "The apartment's great, my job's going well, I'm making friends."

"Where is it you're working?"

Uh-oh. He wasn't going to trip her up again. Her job was much too unique to give him the same answer she'd provided last night. So she went for the most literal reply possible. "Up on Mass Ave. I've become a total city girl, I love taking the Metro train everywhere." She glanced at her watch, pretending she had somewhere to be. "Speaking of which, I'd better run."

"Oh, okay. Well, it was good seeing you."

He actually sounded a little disappointed. Considering he'd just admitted she gave him nightmares, that came as a surprise.

"You, too, Chaz. See ya later."

Hoping she'd come off utterly casual and not the least bit like the mysterious woman he'd met the night before, Lulu walked away as if she actually had somewhere to go.

She felt his eyes on her as she strode toward the end of the block, but managed to avoid looking back. By the time she turned the corner and risked a peek, the street behind her was empty. Maybe she'd just been fooling herself that he had any interest in her at all.

6

LULU.

Lulu Vandenberg.

Lulu Pain-in-the-ass Vandenberg was practically his next-door neighbor. And to make matters worse, for a minute that morning, from a few doors away, he'd thought she was his fantasy woman from last night.

Honestly, Chaz wasn't sure which bothered him more—having somebody who'd tormented him during his geeky, embarrassing younger years so close by, or mistaking that girl for a woman who'd blown his mind while she'd blown *him*.

One thing was for sure—he could never tell Lulu that little tidbit. She'd either laugh in his face…or just slap it. It wasn't nice to have those kinds of thoughts about your parents' best friends' daughter. Or about the girl who'd called you a blockhead for the better part of elementary school.

He managed to hide his snicker when he remembered the new urban slang for the word *blockhead*. It definitely didn't mean what it had meant when they were kids.

In any case, he wasn't going to allow any of those thoughts about Lulu. No way, uh-uh. It had been a simple mistake, quickly made, quickly rectified. He'd mistaken her, okay, *amazing* body for the one he'd been seeking since the previous night. But when he got close enough to see the dark brown hair and the familiar face, he'd shoved such images out of his mind.

That didn't, however, mean the realization that Lulu had grown up to be a very sexy woman was easy to forget. Damn, the girl he'd once known was now a stunner, with those long, dark waves of hair falling well past her shoulders and those heavily-lashed eyes. She had definitely grown up in all the right places, developing the serious curves he'd once teased her she lacked. She now had the kind of body that would make a man drop to his knees and beg for her attention. Her jeans had been simple and faded, but had hugged curvy hips and long, slender legs. And her soft red sweater had emphasized full breasts and a slim waist.

Aside from her sex appeal, she was just beautiful to look at. He'd always thought her pretty, with her thick hair and expressive eyes, at least when she wasn't terrorizing him. But her features had been a little sharp, an impression maybe reinforced by her personality. Now, though, everything had softened, from her face, to her smile, to her voice, to her attitude.

He'd actually enjoyed their brief conversation, and would have liked to continue it. But she'd hurried away from him as quickly as she could. So maybe the long-awaited reunion hadn't been as enjoyable to her as it had been to him.

Which irritated him. She'd always seemed to have the power in their relationship, and it seemed some things never changed.

He was just about to go back to his place when he saw Peggy, his friend and neighbor—and Lulu's—waving from the front door of their building. She gestured him forward.

"Hey, Chaz, can you give us a hand with something?"

"I can try."

"Great. Marcia got a new laptop, and all either of us know about setting it up is pushing the On button."

"I can't guarantee I'll get you much further than that."

"Well, if you can at least get us online so we can stream the newest episode of *Teen Wolf,* we'll pay you back with a steak dinner tomorrow." Peggy wagged her eyebrows up and down and stepped out of the way to let him in the building. "Our pretty neighbor will be joining us. I see you've met her?"

"You mean Lulu?"

"Yeah."

He nodded. "Actually, we've known each other since we were kids."

"Oooh, isn't that interesting?"

"Not particularly." Wanting to nip any matchmaking ideas about him and Lulu in the bud, he asked, "You've lived around here for a few years, right?"

"Yep. We lived one block over until two years ago and right here ever since. Why?"

"I'm just wondering…do you ever remember meeting a really gorgeous redhead? Tall, maybe five-seven, with dark eyes and a great mouth?"

"Hey, I'm a happily married woman."

"I didn't mean for you," he said with a grin.

"Aww, come on, Chaz, you don't need a redhead when you were shooting some serious sparks with our downstairs neighbor."

Lulu? No way, not a chance. He might agree she was sexy, but the only sparks the two of them would set off each other would be if it was the Fourth of July and she stuck a firecracker down his shirt.

"We're just friends. We literally grew up next door to each other."

"Well, isn't it a funny coinkydink, you two ending up as neighbors again. Like fate."

"No, it's not fate. I hooked her up with my Realtor, who works in this area. No hidden meanings or motives. Lulu and I were childhood playmates, and absolutely nothing else."

Playmates, adversaries, same difference.

"Okay," Peggy said with an exaggerated shrug, "If you say so. But I still gotta tell ya, Chaz, from where I was standing, the two of you looked like anything but mere friends."

As if realizing he was uncomfortable, she changed the subject and led him up to the third-floor apartment. Chaz spent a few hours with Peggy and Marcia, helping them set up the new laptop and hook it to their wireless network. He'd never be called a computer genius, but it wasn't too complicated.

Though he didn't, by any means, expect anything for his labors, he ended up accepting their invitation to a cookout the following afternoon. He told himself it had nothing to do with Lulu's presence and wanting to even the score with her. He'd simply been out of the country for a while and looked forward to a last outdoor gathering before the doldrums of winter set in. And he'd probably need to relax and have a few beers with friends after what he expected would be a difficult breakfast with his kid sister.

Besides, spending time with everyone who lived in the building would give him a chance to ask Marcia and the couple from the first floor if they knew a sexy, mysterious redhead. That should hammer home to everyone—including him—the fact that he didn't care at all about Lulu.

The next day turned out better than he'd expected, since

a much more cheerful Sarah had blown off breakfast in favor of a day with friends. So he had plenty of time to unpack and do laundry, and go shopping for this afternoon's gathering.

He arrived a few minutes after four. Peggy had said they were cooking out early to take advantage of the daylight in the rapidly shortening fall day. He headed around to the back of the building, following the sound of voices and laughter. Marcia and Peggy were there, sitting at a picnic table across from a good-looking African-American man. The middle-aged couple who lived on the bottom floor—Florence and Herman? Sherman? something like that—were at the grill, him cooking on it, her telling him how to do it better. They both looked up at him and smiled in greeting.

Lulu sat away from the group, on a garden swing that hung from a tall, leaf-bare tree, pushing off with the tips of her toes to set the thing in motion. Her eyes rounded in surprise when she saw him. "Chaz?"

"Hi, everyone," he said, setting a bottle of wine and a twelve-pack of beer on the table.

"What are you doing here?" she asked, getting up and approaching him, sounding confused, though not exactly unwelcoming.

"Peggy and Marcia invited me."

"Surprise!" said Peggy. "Chaz told me you two were pals from the olden days, and he did us a solid helping us set up our wireless network."

Marcia piped in. "Plus, well, the more the merrier. We wanted to share some news with our friends and neighbors and figured we'd make this a little celebration."

The two women glanced at each other and then Peggy went around to stand behind Marcia, dropping her hands onto her shoulders.

"What's the news?" asked Lulu.

"First, we should introduce Frankie."

The good-looking stranger who'd been sitting at the table smiled and waved as Peggy ran down everyone's names. "Nice meeting y'all."

"Frankie works with Marcia," Peggy explained. "He recently helped us out with a very special project."

"More special than your internet?" Chaz asked with an eyebrow wag.

Peggy's laughter nearly deafened him. "Oh, yeah. You see…we're going to have a baby."

Lulu squealed, as did Florence. Sherman threw his arms up and shouted congratulations in a language that sounded like Italian. Frankie looked proud, and Peggy and Marcia utterly ecstatic.

"Congratulations," Chaz said, smiling at both women. "I can't imagine a kid having better parents."

Lulu rushed around the table and hugged them both, then said, "Okay, now tell me, which one of you *doesn't* get to drink the wine or beer?"

The two women eyed each other mischievously, then both pointed to Marcia's belly. "Seven months without wine, coffee or junk food. I don't know how I'm going to make it."

"I'm going without, too, in solidarity," said Peggy. "Uh, except for the junk food. There's only so much a Nacho Cheese Doritos addict can do to support the woman she loves."

The dinner then segued from a casual neighborhood thing to a celebration. Through it, Chaz watched Lulu, glad to see how totally cool she was with the whole situation. They'd both been raised in a pretty small, conservative town. His own horizons had expanded exponentially after he'd left, and it appeared Lulu's had, too. She was completely gracious and genuinely happy for her new friends.

They all talked and joked through dinner, each offering suggestions for names, one more outrageous than the last. Then, after the steaks were finished and they'd moved on to s'mores for dessert, made over the still smoking grill, Marcia asked, "So, Lulu, what was our Chaz like as a boy?"

Lulu had just sipped a mouthful of wine, and she swallowed quickly, swinging her gaze toward him. He gave a not-so-subtle warning shake of his head.

"Remember, I'm a writer. Any story you can tell, I can tell better," he threatened.

She laughed softly, her brown eyes sparkling in the low light cast from the grill and from a small, warming blaze burning in the fire pit. Her lips were stained red from the wine she'd been drinking, and her hair had blown loose of its ponytail, several strands whipping across her face.

Damn, she was beautiful. If she were anyone else—absolutely *anyone*—she might even be tempting enough to console him over the apparent loss of his mystery woman.

"Well, Chaz was..."

"A loser," he interjected.

She glared at him. "A sweetheart. The nicest boy in town."

He made a rude noise and rolled his eyes. "I don't remember you thinking that when you called me a doody-head because I wouldn't let you ride my new bike on Christmas morning."

"I was five," she said. "And I was the doody-head for assuming you should give up your brand-new bike to the brat next door."

"She's right," said Peggy, obviously amused.

"I might not have told you," Lulu admitted, "but I certainly thought you were the nicest kid I knew." She qualified her answer, offering the group a sheepish smile. "At least…some of the time. Other times, I thought he was a butthead."

He raised his glass. "Here's to the first honest thing you've said."

She raised hers, as well, laughter dancing in her eyes.

After sipping, he jumped in, not wanting her to get the upper hand. "As for Lulu, she was a holy terror."

"No," Marcia protested.

"I don't believe that," said Florence. "She's so quiet, barely a peep from upstairs. I worried when she moved in, thinking such a pretty girl would be bringing the men around at all hours of the night, but there's never a sound from her bedroom, which is right above ours." She reached out and patted Lulu's hand. "She's a good girl."

Color rose in Lulu's cheeks as everyone tried to hide their snorts of laughter. Florence, older and maybe a bit naive, didn't appear to realize her compliment had included a back-handed insult. She looked around in confusion, even as Lulu sunk lower in her seat as everyone speculated on her lack of a sex life.

Chaz caught her eye and offered her a genuine smile. Then he mouthed something only she would understand.

Mwah, mwah, mwah, mwah, mwah.

Their stares locked, and she suddenly laughed with him, the sound infectious, her smile breathtaking.

He was seeing her in a much different light than he'd ever expected to, and he didn't just mean physically, though the physical was definitely potent.

Not that anything could come of it, obviously. The family connection alone would make it impossible for them to try anything beyond friendship, if either of them were interested in that, which he doubted.

When the gathering began to break up, he stayed behind to help clean up. Everybody in the building had brought down something, and then left with what they'd brought. Lulu's contribution had apparently been the plates and silverware. The dishes were all dirty now, and there was no way she could carry all of them up to her place, so he stepped in.

"I'll help Lulu take this up," he offered, clearing one end of the table.

"Thanks, Chaz, we're loaded down," said Peggy. She gestured toward her wife. "And that one's not allowed to carry anything more than a spoon."

Smiling at each other tenderly, the other two women headed inside with platters of leftovers, leaving him and Lulu alone to finish up.

"They're great, aren't they?" she mused.

"Yeah, they're the best," he said. "Peggy and Marcia were the first neighbors I met when I moved in, and they helped me unpack boxes for a week."

"They did the same thing for me. I appreciated the help—and I appreciate yours now," she said. "I'd hate to make three trips since I live on the second floor."

He could have been nice and not taken a swing at the pitch she'd thrown. But he just couldn't resist. "Yeah, I heard you lived on the second floor. Your room is right above Florence's."

She scowled and threw a wadded-up napkin in his face.

"Okay, sorry, I didn't hear a word Florence said," he claimed with a wicked grin.

"As if she'd hear anything, anyway," Lulu said, tossing her head, which shook free her ponytail, sending her dark hair tumbling down her back. "I happen to have a very new bed with quiet springs."

He supposed she was trying to salvage her pride, but he wasn't focused on that. For some reason, the idea of Lulu bouncing around in bed with a man was enough to make him stop laughing.

It's just because you're not used to thinking of her as a grown woman. You're still picturing the girl next door, the one who wore angel's wings and a halo in her second grade Christmas pageant, making all the other kids laugh because Lulu was anything but angelic.

Yeah. That was it. Totally.

It had nothing to do with her delicious-looking body, that amazing mouth, all that thick, dark hair that he could suddenly envision being spread across his naked stomach.

Jeez, he really needed to get a grip. More, he needed to find the woman he'd met Friday night. Sexual frustration was making him think the craziest thoughts about someone he should never consider in that way.

"I could give Florence something to listen to," she muttered, still obviously disgruntled about her neighbor's comments. "Something that would have her reaching for her earplugs and praying for my soul."

"Gonna download porn from the internet and set the speaker by the air vent?"

She glared at him. "Some men actually find me attractive, you know."

He didn't doubt it. Physically, she was mouthwatering. It was the nonphysical part that was the problem.

"And I don't need porn."

"Nobody *needs* porn," he said philosophically. "But it can be kinda fun on occasion."

She licked her lips, her lashes dropping over those brown eyes. "Speaking from experience?" she asked, her voice probably not as cool and noncommittal as she'd been going for.

He kept his answer just as cool. "Maybe."

"And here I pegged you as the big stud, women in every town."

He couldn't believe they were having this conversation, but since they were, he decided to finish it. "Porn's not just for lonely guys who have no friends other than Hairy Palmer." Remembering the highlights from Friday night, he added, "You've never thought about watching other people have sex? Or of being watched yourself?"

"You mean, intentional exhibitionism?"

He nodded. She caught her lip between her teeth and shook her head violently. "Never," she swore, though he suspected she was lying to them both.

He had, on occasion, enjoyed watching sex, via hotel movie rentals and adventurous internet surfing. But until the other night in that savings and loan lobby, and then later up against that tree, he'd never even dreamed of someone watching him with a woman. That night had been so wild, so uninhibited and dangerous, he'd half wanted to be caught.

Chaz had never considered himself an exhibitionist, had never toyed with the idea of allowing strangers to peek in on his life, especially during his most personal moments. But somehow, he almost got off on the idea of laying the most earthy, sexual claim on a woman—*that* woman— while others stood watching in envy.

Deep down, the ancient caveman within him wanted to put his mark on her, to proclaim that she was his, and warn every other man not to trespass. He wanted to pleasure her, do wild, erotic things to her that nobody would ever even dare try to repeat because they knew he'd set a bar so high it could never be surpassed. He wanted to show off, to prove he was the ultimate lover so she'd never dream of being with anyone else.

It was sexist, it would probably piss off most women, but it was entirely true.

He didn't think it would anger his mystery witch, though. She'd seemed just as into it as he was. Maybe that was one reason why he so wanted to find her again... to see if she shared the fantasy and wanted to finish what they'd started. In public, in private, it didn't matter. He just wanted to have her.

"Here," Lulu said, interrupting his heated musings by shoving a trio of dirty plates in his hands. "Get your mind out of the gutter."

"You brought it up."

"I most certainly did not!"

"You're the one who mentioned bouncy bedsprings."

"Oh, shut up."

Laughter on his lips at how easy she was to rile, he followed her inside and up the back stairs. A few steps below her, he found himself eye level with an amazing ass and wished he hadn't just been picturing such graphic thoughts.

When, he wondered, had Lulu become so thoroughly feminine? She had curves on top of curves, and he couldn't tear his stare off those amazing hips and thighs as he followed two steps behind her. Thinking about porn and voyeurism and sex ninety seconds before being presented face-to-butt with pure temptation was not a good thing for any guy. Especially not if he wanted to keep his jeans lying flat against his groin.

His weren't.

Holy shit. They *weren't*.

He was hard for Lulu. If he were to be honest about it, he'd have to admit he'd started getting hard when she'd made that crack about her bedsprings.

This was unacceptable on so many levels, he couldn't even begin to count them. Lulu had made his life hell, she was trouble, she was a part of his past that he didn't much care to revisit. He had no business imagining her body or her bed or anything else.

On the top step, she swung around and caught him staring.

"I knew you were looking at my ass," she said, typical blunt Lulu.

He couldn't even try to deny it. Hell, all she had to do was glance down and see the bulge in his jeans and she'd prove him a liar. Which meant he needed to keep her attention focused above his waist.

"Guilty. You definitely grew up." He stepped up beside her, forcing himself to smile down at her. "When'd that happen?"

"When you weren't looking."

He was looking now, though he shouldn't be. He couldn't even figure out why he wanted to. This was *Lulu* of all people! The girl had poured an entire milkshake over his head once because he'd asked her if she'd been crying. He had no doubt she'd do the same thing again today if she had the chance.

"I somehow suspect you forgot who you were talking to and who you were ogling," she whispered, blinking those dark eyes—familiar eyes, beautiful eyes—and staring searchingly at his face.

"Maybe I did, for just a minute."

Some instinct he couldn't define made him reach up to smooth back a strand of her long, dark hair, which was wind-whipped and soft against his fingers. His fingertips brushed against her cheekbone, and he realized her skin was equally as soft, her peaches-and-cream complexion revealing a flush of color in her face.

Her tongue flicked out and she moistened her lips, exhaling a long, slow breath as the lingering stare continued.

He was hit with the strangest feeling of déjà vu. It was ridiculous, really, because he'd never touched her like this. He'd never even dreamed he might someday have the impulse to lean in and taste that sassy, saucy mouth, to kiss the insults right out of it.

And yet he did.

He suddenly wanted to kiss her, wanted to experience that lush mouth against his own. He wanted to press her soft, curvy body against his and wanted to explore every inch of her.

Of Lulu. Lulu Vandenberg.

"Lulu," he whispered, feeling himself lean closer, drawn by something irresistible and irrevocable, as if he had no strength of will.

Their faces came close. Their lips nearly touched.

Then she took a step back and grabbed the dishes out of his hands. "I can handle it from here."

He blinked, shaking his head hard, wondering whether he'd fallen under some magic spell. How else could he possibly explain his desire to do something as insane as kiss a girl he'd barely tolerated for most of his life?

"Thanks for the help," she said, stepping across the small hallway to the door of her place. "I'll see you later."

Not waiting for him to reply, she twisted the unlocked knob and stepped into her apartment. She shut the door hard, the audible flipping of the lock from within punctuating what she'd been saying to him.

Good night. Goodbye. Go away.

"You're welcome," he whispered. "Goodbye."

He would swear he heard her shuddery exhalation from inside. Chaz sensed she stood right on the other side of the door, resting her head against it, uncomfortable, unsure.

How very unlike her.

He turned to do exactly as she wanted. He would go away. For now, at least.

But not forever.

Because something had occurred to him when she'd reacted so anxiously to their unexpected chemistry. For some reason, having him around made her nervous. The situation unsettled her far more than it did him. Which meant for once in their long history, he had the advantage.

How interesting to finally have gained an advantage over Lulu Vandenberg.

And how fun it might be to use that advantage to drive her absolutely insane.

7

ALTHOUGH LULU TRIED to keep her mind off Chaz, mere proximity made it impossible. Over the next several days, she ran into him every single morning. It was as if fate kept putting him in her path. Or, well, their work schedules did.

They both left at around the same time every weekday, and both rode the Metro to their respective places of employment. That meant they walked to the station together, waited together, even rode together for a few stops. They talked, at least as much as two coffee addicts could manage to talk at seven in the morning.

And both of them put on a pretty good front, as if they didn't really mind being thrown into each other's company so much, even though she, at least, definitely did. Because being with Chaz—even when she was bleary-eyed and coffee-deprived, focused on work and the shitty commute and the rush of people in the city—still excited her altogether too much for her peace of mind.

She just couldn't go back to thinking of him as good old Chaz. Not when she'd spent one wicked evening with the man, a man more sexually exciting than any she'd ever known. The attraction was eating at her, the pressure to keep her secret intensely frustrating. Every time she saw

Chaz swing his head around to catch a glimpse at a passing redhead, she wanted to stomp on his foot, grab his face and order him to look at *her.*

Yes, she'd been masked, yes her hair had been sprayed a different color, yes she'd intentionally tried to change the tone of her voice, but still, couldn't he recognize her scent? The shape of her mouth? The hands, the body, the laugh? Jesus, she would be able to pick him out in a packed stadium, even if she'd never met him before Halloween night, and the fact that he hadn't even begun to connect her to his mystery witch was driving her a little nutty.

She'd told herself she was being stupid, since evading detection was absolutely necessary. But that hadn't helped much. The more her frustration built, the more she realized she needed to steer clear of him.

Hoping to do just that, she'd tried to leave earlier one day…and so had he. She'd wondered if he was trying to avoid her, too. Neither of them admitted it, and he probably felt as dumb as she did. As far as he was concerned, they were old neighbors for heaven's sake, there should be no reason they couldn't chat comfortably.

Well, except for the part that he'd fingered her to an orgasm and she'd sucked his big, hard cock as if it was the world's tastiest peppermint stick. But he didn't know that.

Thankfully, on Saturday she had a break. She wouldn't have to spend another morning pretending to seek nothing but long-standing friendship for a guy whose body filled her fantasies and whose mouth made her weak in the knees—and who would hate her guts when he found out the truth.

She slept in that morning, but her internal clock wouldn't let her stay asleep any later than nine. Getting up, she deliberately bounced the springs of her bed, and stepped a little heavier on her hardwood floors. Now that she was aware Florence was downstairs listening, she felt the need to put up a brave, false front. Hell, did the entire building really have to discuss her sex life…or lack thereof? Oh, that moment had been embarrassing. Bless Chaz for knowing exactly what to do to get her past her immediate humiliation by making her laugh.

Chaz the savior, Chaz the sweetheart, Chaz the good guy. How could she ever have considered him Chaz the loser? She must have been the one with rocks in her head.

Needing to get completely out of the neighborhood today, she was grateful for another weekend of unseasonably warm weather. It wasn't quite as nice as last weekend had been, when she hadn't even required a jacket. Still, it was pleasant enough for some outdoor activities, and she knew how she would spend her afternoon.

In good weather, some of her coworkers and other city residents got together for kickball games near the Washington Monument every other weekend. A coworker had left her a message last night, saying today would be the last game of the year, and urging her to come. Wanting the company and the exercise, and needing the distraction, she'd agreed. She knew better than to ask her two closest friends, Viv and Amelia, to join in. Viv's only physical activity was having sex, and Amelia always worked at her craft shop on Saturdays. Still, it should be fun to work off some energy with some newer friends.

Donning athletic clothes and her sneakers, she headed outside. Turning right would take her down to the Metro station, but would also send her right past Chaz's front door. He was probably busy, almost certainly wouldn't be looking out the window, and, even if he did, and if he saw her, he definitely wouldn't come out to talk to her. He probably felt stalked after their daily interactions during the work week.

But…she turned left anyway. She was taking the long way around, adding a couple of blocks to her walk, but it was worth it, if only for her peace of mind.

"Tell me the truth, are you following me or did you plant a tracking device in my jacket?"

Shocked when she heard a familiar voice, she looked to the entrance of a small cafe on the corner, seeing a very familiar man emerging from within.

"Chaz?"

"Hello, Lulu."

"What are you doing here?"

"I just came out to grab a late breakfast. What are *you* doing here?"

"I'm on my way to the station."

His brow furrowed in confusion and he pointed back the way she'd come. "The station's that way."

She scrambled for a suitable retort. "I mean, well, I wanted to grab a sports drink, then I'm heading to the station."

"Believe it or not, that's where I'm going, too," he said with a helpless shrug. "Where are you off to?"

"Up to the Mall for a game of kickball."

His jaw dropped open. "Seriously?"

Sudden foreboding made her tense. "Yes. Why?"

Shaking his head slowly, he replied, "Well, I'm going to the same place, for the same reason."

Lulu's stomach churned. This wasn't going to be the quick hello-and-goodbye she'd envisioned. "Really?"

"Yep. I'm in an informal league. We play softball in the spring when a lot of people are around. It's more laid-back in the fall and we play kickball for fun. I heard some people were putting together a late-season game and said I'd play."

"Oh. I guess smart minds think alike. I played a few times earlier in the fall, and got asked to come today, too."

Of course, Chaz hadn't been at those previous games, since he'd been out of the country. She cursed her luck, wanting nothing more than to escape him before she did something stupid, like ask, "Hey, still searching in vain for a redhead with an ass you wanted to nibble on?"

She didn't, of course, and mentally slapped herself for even imagining him using that beautiful mouth on any sensitive part of her anatomy. She'd had enough wet dreams over the man this past week, not that any of them could compare to the real moments they'd shared in that ATM vestibule.

They were both silent for a moment, then Chaz said, "So, want to go up to the Mall together?"

Always the nice guy. He'd probably rather be anywhere else, with anyone else. But since she couldn't come up with a logical reason to decline, she merely nodded.

"I'll wait here if you want to go inside and grab a drink."

Again, she couldn't think of any way to refuse. Nodding, she stepped into the café, which sold bottled drinks, and grabbed the first one she could reach. She paid, carried it back outside, smiled and said, "Okay, ready to go?"

"That's not a sports drink."

She glanced at the bottle in her hand and realized she'd picked up a container of milk. Good grief, that was the last thing she needed to drink before running around playing a physical game.

Especially since she hated milk.

"Aren't you going to drink up?" he asked, a sparkle of mischief in his eye.

Damn it, Chaz knew she hated milk. He'd badgered her often enough about the fact that she liked it over cereal, but wouldn't drink a glass unless she plugged her nose, and she still gagged as it went down.

"No, uh, I think I'll save it for later."

"Don't wait too long, it might curdle."

Yeah, so might her stomach if she tried to drink the stuff.

As they walked to the station, they passed some people with faces that were becoming familiar to her. Dupont Circle was a small part of a big city, and there was a strong sense of community here.

Chaz was friendly to everyone they passed, several of whom appeared to know him. She noted a lot of women gave him appreciative looks, and she suddenly found herself stepping a little closer to him on the cobbled walkway. Close enough that their legs brushed. That faint contact was all it took to remind her of the erotic moments they'd shared the weekend before, and she quickly stepped away.

But perhaps not quickly enough. Chaz was eyeing her, an inscrutable expression on his face. He appeared confused by something. She had to wonder if his own sense memories were working on him, trying to force the truth of her identity into his brain. Wouldn't that be about damn time?

And while she knew that would be the absolute worst thing that could happen in the long run, part of her was very interested in finding out just how Chaz Browning would react if he learned that the woman he'd been seeking had been right under his nose the whole time.

AFTER A WEEK of enforced proximity, Chaz probably shouldn't have suggested that he and Lulu head up to the Mall together. He'd had fun making her a little crazy this week by always making sure they bumped into each other on the way to work or when walking the neighborhood, but he didn't want to push her too far. Actually, when she'd mentioned where she was going, he should have kept his mouth shut about being en route to the same place, and found another way to spend the day.

What he should have said, however, and what he *had* said, were two different things. He wanted to spend the day in the company of the woman he couldn't stop thinking about…in good ways, and in bad.

Because a funny thing had happened during his campaign to rile her up this week—he'd realized he enjoyed being with her. Lulu had changed a lot. Her demeanor was down-to-earth and approachable. She joked around, but there was no real snark. She was just friendly and funny, never going for a dig when a quip would do, her voice holding no edge, her smile no malice.

And Lulu was certainly not hard to look at—sexy and appealing, even when dressed in sports clothes. Hell, *especially* when dressed in sports clothes. Spandex did amazing things for that already amazing ass and those legs.

If only she were anyone but the devil-next-door.

As they took the Metro up to the Mall, getting off at the Smithsonian station and walking past the Washington Monument down to the grassy area where the teams usually played, he and Lulu traded stories about kids they'd known and teachers they'd disliked. They had even laughed over some shared memories.

One topic that did not come up was their siblings. Damn, he did not want Sarah to find out Lulu lived right up the street from him. His hotheaded sister might march to her door and demand that Lulu do something about Lawrence, as if she had the right to order her high school boyfriend out of the nation's capital. But other than avoiding that subject, he and Lulu fell into an easy camaraderie that had been hinted at but never fully realized during their childhood.

Of course, that camaraderie all but disappeared during the game, when they realized they were on opposite teams. Lulu was as competitive as always, while Chaz, who showed up to these games mostly to hang out with friends, barely paid attention to the score.

"Come on, Browning, are you gonna kick it or sit on it?" Lulu called from the pitcher's mound, her tone pissy.

It was his turn to kick, but he'd taken his sweet time getting to home plate. He'd been talking with a colleague, Tonia, an attractive blonde with whom he'd shared a couple of interesting nights a couple of years ago. No sizzle remained between them, but he still liked her well enough.

"We don't have all day."

Lulu's almost angry tone made him finally give his full attention to the game. "Who made *you* pitcher?" he asked, watching her lean over to line up her rolling pitch.

"She's got a mean throw, dude, watch out," said one of his teammates, who'd apparently gone up against Lulu before.

"Chaz knows all about how mean I am," said Lulu, her smile appearing forced. She cast a quick, quelling look at Tonia, then got her head back in the game.

Lulu was all business when she pitched, whipping the rubber ball straight at him. It bounced twice before rolling fast and hard, directly toward the plate, where he met it with the broad side of his right foot. The ball flew up and over the entire field, down into a group of kids playing tag. No way would anybody get it back up here before he rounded all the bases.

As he jogged around the field, he caught Lulu's eye and grinned at her dour expression. "Guess I shoulda warned you," he called, laughter in his voice. "I'm not so bad at sports anymore."

"Does that mean I can actually be on your softball team in the spring and not worry we'll lose one-hundred to nothing?" she asked, her tone sugar-sweet, though her eyes were hard.

Her zinger just amused him even more, and his laughter rang out, simple and joyful. He laughed at her, and at the bright, sunny morning. He thoroughly enjoyed the feeling of being back in a place where he could appreciate a beautiful day like this without a pervading sense of fear or uncertainty.

Maybe someday he'd stop feeling the need to head off to one hotspot or another. At times like this, he could actually envision it. Hell, if he had the right person to make him want to stay, he might never get the urge to leave again.

The thought killed his laughter. He might already have found—and lost—the woman of his dreams on Halloween night. Well, maybe not of his dreams, but she was definitely the woman of his fantasies.

Most of them.

Yeah. Most of them. He wasn't about to admit to anyone—including himself—that Lulu had appeared in some pretty vivid mental pictures on a couple of occasions this week. She and the mysterious redhead both haunted him. That was crazy, since one was an old enemy and he didn't know the name of the other. Nor did he have any idea why she'd run out on him.

Thinking back on their evening, he forced himself to remember the number of times she'd tried to dance away, or put up barriers between them. She'd been on guard, making it clear she was only willing to go so far.

Maybe he'd pushed too hard and scared her off. Maybe she'd been afraid she'd come across too strong. Maybe she had a deathly fear of waffles. Whatever it was, something had made her change her mind. He simply wasn't going to rest until he knew who she was and why she'd left.

After the game, everyone headed for a nearby bar for

midafternoon libations. Chaz walked with Tonia, while Lulu fell into step beside Darrell, a guy on Lulu's team. Chaz tensed, remembering Darrell was often called a pig by some of the women because he was such a player.

Lulu probably didn't know that, however, being so new to the area. Whatever the guy was saying to her had to be hilarious because she laughed like she was sitting in the front row of a Def Comedy Jam. Chaz kept his eyes on the back of her head, noting the jaunty bounce of her ponytail, a frown tugging at his mouth.

"What's wrong?" asked Tonia.

"Nothing," he insisted, not wanting to admit yet that the sight of Lulu so enjoying another guy's company bugged him.

His goal had been to drive Lulu crazy, not himself. But now, watching her looking up at Darrell, with a big smile on that beautiful mouth, all he could remember was that moment last weekend when he'd stood outside her door, brushed her hair off her face and wondered what it would be like to kiss her.

"How was your first week back?"

"Not bad," he replied, finally tearing his attention off his distracting neighbor. "I completed the first draft of part one of a series and sent it to editing. The powers-that-be seem to like it and are expecting a wide distribution."

He'd written several short articles while overseas, all of them distributed by the Associated Press and picked up by news outlets all over the world. But he'd also been asked to do an in-depth series with a narrower focus. They were to be longer pieces—five-thousand words—that could end up featured in one of the big print outlets. He sure wouldn't mind a *Time* magazine spot at this point in his career.

"How about you?"

Tonia frowned. "I'm still working on an exposé of that scam charity organization."

"What was that about again?" he asked, not remembering the details, which she'd mentioned to him the last time they'd talked, before his trip.

"It's one of those give-microloans-to-African-mothers things." Tonia sneered. "Another group of bleeding heart do-gooders trying to change the world, twenty-five dollars at a time."

"Those groups make a big difference in some parts of the world."

She rolled her eyes and waved a hand, obviously unwilling to even consider that she might be wrong. "Give me a break. I'm *sure* there's something dirty going on there, I just know it. But it's taking me a while to find it."

Chaz came to a sudden stop, turning to look at her. He suddenly remembered his conversation with his mystery woman, who'd talked about having a job just like that one. There couldn't be that many of those types of NGOs in Washington, could there?

He might have found a solid clue in tracking her down.

"I'm interested in hearing more," he said, meaning it. "Sit with me at the bar and tell me everything you've uncovered, okay?"

Tonia licked her lips as she slid her arm in his and they resumed walking. Something about her expression sent a warning through his brain. God, he hoped she didn't think he was just making excuses to be with her, in hopes of reviving their fling.

Because his mystery witch suddenly seemed more within reach than ever. Which put a spring in his step and an anticipatory smile on his face.

When they got to the bar, the group spread out, taking up several tables. Everyone ordered beers and sandwiches, chatting loudly and making plans for the spring season. As promised, he sat with Tonia, feeling her out for information on the NGO she was researching, which was called Hands Across The Waters. He took mental notes, determined to research the group as soon as he got home. They might have a staff directory on their website, might even have pictures. He could feel himself edging closer and closer to solving the mystery.

But even as she filled him in, he kept glancing at a table by the door, where Lulu sat with Darrell, and a new arrival. Schaefer, who didn't play kickball, or do much of anything except pluck the strings of a guitar, had joined in. Apparently he was friends with one of the other players, who'd invited him to come over.

Lulu looked as pleased as punch to be sitting between the two men, both of whom were chatting her up. Honestly, Chaz had never seen Schaefer so animated. Or Darrell appearing so innocent.

"So, this Lulu chick," Tonia said with a frown, "I take it you know her?"

He tore his attention off the trio at the other table. "What?"

"Come on, you haven't taken your eyes off her since the two of you got to the game."

"We go back a ways. Grew up together."

"Ah. So you feel brotherly, huh? Because you looked like you wanted to go over there and rip Darrell's arm off when he put it around her."

"He's so sleazy," Chaz said, his jaw tightening. And the very idea that he felt brotherly toward Lulu was just ridiculous.

"I don't know, I always thought he was pretty hot, and that he'd straighten up for the right woman." Tonia toyed with the condensation on her glass. "Maybe he thinks she's the one?"

That thought just made Chaz's annoyance increase. He couldn't help grumbling, "That booth's plenty big, he did not need to put his arm around her and pull her closer to make room for Schaefer." He took another gulp of his beer. "And is there any reason Schaefer couldn't have sat across from her, rather than next to her?"

"There's another guy sitting across from her."

"What sense does that make, three on one side of the table, one on the other?"

His companion sighed deeply. "How long ago did you two break up?"

He almost spit out his mouthful of beer. "Lulu and I have *never* been a couple."

She didn't appear convinced. "Uh-huh. Sure."

"No, seriously. She is the last woman in the world I'd even think about getting involved with."

"Right."

"She was the bane of my childhood. Our parents are best friends—they went through hell when my sister and Lulu's brother made the mistake of getting involved and then breaking up. I'd never put any of us through that again."

"Okay, okay, I get it," said Tonia, lifting her own drink. Before she sipped it, she added, "But remember that old adage about the guy who protested too much? Well, look in the mirror, dude. 'Cause that's you."

He wasn't quite ready to admit that her reporter instincts were spot on. But before he could even open his mouth, he got a glimpse under the other table and saw Darrell drop a hand onto Lulu's thigh and squeeze it. He was up out of his seat, a growl on his lips, before his brain even engaged.

Fortunately, he came to his senses. Or, Lulu came to

hers. She immediately asked Schaefer to get out of the way and removed herself from Darrell's obnoxious grip. Giving him a withering glare that would reduce any guy to a tiny kernel of male ego, she excused herself and headed toward the back of the place, obviously looking for the ladies' room.

Schaefer made some kind of comment to Darrell, then got up and followed Lulu.

Chaz didn't think about it. Something wouldn't let him sit back down and allow Lulu to handle her own affairs. Mumbling an excuse to Tonia, he strode across the place, toward the hallway through which the others had disappeared.

Schaefer was hovering around outside the ladies' room door.

"Is there a line?" Chaz asked, nodding toward the men's.

The guy flushed and swallowed. "Oh, uh, no, go ahead."

He crossed his arms and jutted out his jaw. "You first."

Unable or unwilling to admit he'd been stalking Lulu, the other man ducked into the men's room, leaving Chaz alone in the dark, shadowy corridor. He stood there just long enough to ask himself what the hell he was doing when the ladies' room door opened and Lulu stepped out.

"Oh, Chaz! You startled me."

"Are you all right?"

She nodded, reaching up to tuck a strand of hair behind her ear. It was a little messy from the game. Her cheeks were high with color, her eyes bright, yet, altogether, she looked about as good as he'd ever seen her.

She affected him, deep inside, as all his protective instincts combined with his most covetous ones. He wanted to shield her from some horny guy because she deserved better…but also, he suddenly realized, because he wanted her for himself!

It was totally insane and unacceptable. Sure, he might have been flirting with her this past week to make her sweat, but he'd never intended it to go this far.

Still, he couldn't bring himself to just walk away and pretend he didn't care about what had happened.

"I'm fine, thanks."

"Is the pig bothering you?"

"Who?"

"Darrell. I saw him touch you."

Her lips tightened. "And you felt the need to, what, play overprotective older brother? I'm not Sarah, you know."

"The guy's a creep."

"I'm a big girl."

"I'm just giving you fair warning. You can't trust him."

"You think the third grope under the table didn't tip me off to that?"

Steam built in his head. "Third? He groped you three times? I only noticed him touch your leg."

She crossed her arms over her chest. "That's not surprising. I mean, how could you have been paying close attention to what I was doing when you were so busy trying to score with that ditzy blonde who's been hanging all over you?"

It was his turn to gape in surprise. "What?"

"Come on, Chaz, don't act like you don't know what I'm talking about," she said, edging closer until the tips of her sneakers touched his. "She acted like a toddler learning to walk during the game. *Oh, Chaz, would you teach little old me how to kick like that?* Gag me."

Tension and anger sparked between them, creating a nearly electric current. It crackled between their bodies, and he noticed her chest was heaving with anger and emotion as she struggled to control her breathing.

"Who's the pot and who's the kettle here?" he said,

inching even closer, until one of his legs was between hers and their hips grazed. He ignored that, towering over her. "Sounds to me as if you're projecting your own behavior."

"I'm not shaking my tail under some guy's nose and playing the poor-hopeless-girl-can't-kick-a-ball role to try to get his attention," she snarled, not backing down one inch.

They were so close, they shared each breath. Fire snapped in her eyes, and her voice shook with emotion.

"No, you're just playing the creamy filling for a guy sandwich, sitting between two dudes who've been taking turns looking down your shirt."

She gasped audibly, and fisted her hand to punch him. Typical Lulu. Chaz instinctively reacted, reaching up and grabbing her wrist before she could take a swing.

They glared at each other for a loaded moment, and then, somehow, their mouths were together and they were kissing with anger-driven hunger.

Chaz didn't think, didn't plan. He acted on tension and instinct, just wanting to shut her up, to win the argument, to taste her and stop the crazy wondering that had been tormenting him since last week when he'd followed her up the stairs to her apartment.

He moaned, or she did, and suddenly her arms were around his neck, her fingers tangling in his hair and holding him tight. He dragged her body against his, lifting her off her feet and wrapping his arms around her waist. Their tongues tangled wildly as they gave and took, demanded and received.

The kiss affected him from head to toe. The feel of her soft, curvy form against his drove him slightly mad, and he pushed her up against the wall, loving the way her legs instinctively snaked around his until he was supporting her entire weight. The spandex was slick in his hands, but he had no problem gripping her taut ass, hoisting her even higher until they were lined up at just the perfect angle for wild, intense, up-against-the-wall sex, just as he'd envisioned having on Halloween night.

It made no sense. That night, he'd been with a stranger who'd driven him wild with lust. But this was Lulu, a girl he'd known forever. How could she possibly be even more exciting, more arousing to him than his masked mystery woman?

Kissing Lulu was like leaping willingly into a volcano, aware you might get burned but also sure you'd be in for a hell of a ride when it erupted. It was pure, raw excitement, born out of anger, but quickly exploding into sexual frenzy.

Only the fact that they were erupting in a bar filled with their friends finally brought him to his senses. He ended the kiss, releasing her and staggering back one step. She did the same, her eyes wide and wild, her face red and her whole body quivering. She looked shocked and aroused, but her expression quickly segued into embarrassed confusion.

"What the hell was that?"

He thrust a hand through his hair, which was tangled from her tight grip. "Damn it, Lulu, I didn't mean…"

"Don't. Just don't say another word. This is bad enough."

"Uh, is there a problem?"

They both jerked their attention to the side and saw Schaefer, who'd just emerged from the men's room.

"No, there's no problem," Lulu insisted.

"I don't mean to intrude," the other guy said, "but Lulu, you seem upset."

"I'm fine."

"Are you sure? I could…"

"Back off, Ludwig," Chaz snapped.

Schaefer's eyes rounded into circles and his pale face lost what little color it had held. His spine stiffened, and he looked as though he had been slapped. Chaz closed his eyes, dropping his head, feeling like a complete heel. What the hell was it about Lulu that made all his brain cells dry up and blow away?

Lulu had obviously heard. *"Ludwig?"*

"You dick," Schaefer said, glaring at Chaz before pushing past them and heading straight to the exit. Chaz knew he owed the guy an apology, since he'd promised not to reveal his real name. But right now, that goofy name, and Schaefer's swishy diva walkout, relieved the tension and enabled him and Lulu to recover from their crazy kiss.

She broke first, starting to snicker, and then to laugh.

Equally relieved, Chaz joined her in the laughter. "He's never gonna forgive me."

"His first name is Ludwig? *Seriously?*"

He nodded. "Yeah, I think his parents had a Beethoven fetish along with their hippie lifestyle."

"Poor guy," Lulu said, leaning back against the wall, her laughter fading until just a faint smile remained. "No wonder he goes by his last name and keeps the first one a secret."

When a more comfortable silence descended, he murmured, "Lulu, I'm sorry."

She didn't look at him, merely nodding. "Me, too. That should definitely never have happened."

She was a little too quick to agree that they had no business kissing.

Of course, she was right. He'd wanted to get to know her again, but they did have no business kissing, or doing anything else, for that matter. Not only was there the family issue, there was also the fact that Lulu was new to D.C., soaking up every experience she could get, dedicated to her new job and her friends. She was starting the whole single-in-the-city phase, and the last thing she needed would be to get seriously involved with anyone—especially someone who jetted around the world without even telling his loved ones when he was heading into a war zone.

And he just couldn't see them being involved casually. He might fantasize about taking her home and having steamy sex with her, but considering she lived a few doors down, it sure would make for some awkward mornings after. Not to mention some tense trips home for the holidays. He could just envision the two of them sitting with both their families around a Christmas tree, trying to pretend they hadn't explored every inch of each other's bodies with their mouths.

His own went dry at the very thought of it.

No. Not happening.

He had to forget it and move on. She'd been right the first time when she'd shut the door in his face. There was no point in even thinking about that kiss again…even though he was damn sure he would never forget it.

Their stares locked, and Chaz managed to keep his focus strictly on her eyes. He didn't drop his gaze to those well-kissed lips, or to the amazing body all hugged by spandex.

"Things are way too tangled for us to even consider letting this go anywhere," she said, reading his mind.

"Yeah. Momentary insanity."

"Definitely."

"Never to be repeated."

"Absolutely not. God, if things got so bad with Sarah and Lawrence, can you imagine how it would be for us?"

He didn't really appreciate the comparison, considering their siblings had gone through their nonsense as high-schoolers, but he understood the sentiment. "It could be bad" was as far as he was willing to go.

It could also be good. But neither of them was ready to find out.

"So it can't go anywhere." A tiny sigh preceded her next comment, and she suddenly looked wistful. "I finally feel like you and I are starting to be friends, Chaz. I don't want to screw that up."

That hadn't exactly been his intention, but he agreed. While they'd known each other forever, they had never *really* been friends. Lately, it had seemed as if they'd begun moving in that direction. He didn't want to screw that up, either.

"We won't. For once, I appreciate your directness. I hate playing games. We'll just forget this happened, go back to our own private lives and back to being old childhood..."

"Combatants?"

Her joke lifted the tension even more.

"Something like that."

Agreed, they took another moment to ease back into this new version of normal, then they turned and exited the hallway, heading toward their friends and teammates. Chaz watched her beeline for another table, taking a seat beside one of the women on her team. Darrell, he noticed, had stood up and was lurking near the door. When he saw Lulu choose another table, he ducked out of the bar without any goodbyes. Which was for the best...it meant Chaz wouldn't have to threaten his life or anything.

Not out of jealousy, of course. But because friends looked out for each other.

Friends. Just friends.

He sat back at his own table, ignoring Tonia's curious

stare questioning why he'd been gone so long, and flagged down the waitress for his check. Chaz just wasn't interested in having another beer or socializing. He was too confused to relax and enjoy himself. Confused over that kiss, how he'd reacted to it, and how it had compared to the ones he'd exchanged to the woman haunting his dreams.

Lulu was as familiar to him as a family member, dark-haired, sassy-mouthed, not mysterious. The witch he'd met on Halloween had been entirely different.

So why was he having such a hard time separating them in his mind? And why did the memory of Lulu's kiss have him so on edge and curious?

He just didn't know. He needed to go home and think things through before he found reasons to ignore every decision he'd made regarding Lulu.

Then, something happened that changed everything. The door to the bar opened, bringing in a strong autumn breeze, some dried, tumbling leaves, and three women. A brunette, a blonde, and…

"A redhead," he murmured, unable to tear his eyes off the woman in the middle. The tall one with the long, wind-blown hair, and the dark eyes.

His heart skipped a beat. He blinked, staring at her again, wishing he were closer.

He couldn't be sure, not until he talked to her—heard her voice, got a better look at her mouth. After all, Washington, D.C. was a big city. There had to be thousands of attractive women with red hair. Tens of thousands.

But stranger things had happened.

Maybe fate was tossing him a bone after he'd experienced that momentary insanity with Lulu, and then intelligently agreed to never repeat it. Perhaps his luck was turning. A week ago, the mysterious woman he'd met on Halloween night had captured his full attention. It was now time to put his focus back where it belonged—on a woman who'd intrigued him, who'd wanted him, and who must have had a damn good reason for leaving the way she had.

Not on the woman he'd just agreed he could never—*ever*—have.

8

"HER NAME IS HEATHER, and he thinks she's me. And she apparently is *letting* him think that. Could you just die?"

Lulu threw herself back in her chair, swallowing a big mouthful of wine, waiting for her friends to start commiserating and giving her lots of *You go girl!*s.

They didn't.

Viv merely watched her with a half smirk on her full lips, and Amelia wore a look of sad disapproval.

The three of them had met at a restaurant near Viv's place in Georgetown, Lulu badly needing a girls' night out after the way things had been going the past couple of weeks. She wanted her friends to be indignant on her behalf and rain curses on the evil Heather's head, and do all the things girlfriends were supposed to do when one of them was feeling betrayed.

And she was definitely feeling betrayed.

Men could be so totally dense. Especially when they were being led around by their dicks.

After that insanely erotic, wonderful, sexy kiss she and Chaz had shared, he'd agreed that they couldn't let things go any further, and had gone right back to obsessing over the redhead he'd met on Halloween night.

Which was Lulu.

Only she couldn't let him know that.

And now he thought the redhead he'd met minutes after that wonderful, erotic kiss was his mysterious Halloween witch.

It was too confusing to dwell on for long. All she knew was, the witch—literally speaking, only in her mind she usually referred to Heather with the *b*-word instead—had apparently not made it clear to him that she wasn't the woman he'd been searching for. The two of them appeared to be getting very cozy. *Grr.*

"He even invited her for Thanksgiving dinner, can you freaking believe it?"

That should definitely have earned a few *That skank, bet she's not even a real redhead* comments from her gal pals. But she didn't get them.

"You have to tell him the truth," Amelia said, her pretty blue eyes warm and supportive.

Amelia was the nicest young woman Lulu had ever met. She never had a mean word to say to anyone, and probably did a lousy business of running her craft shop because she believed every sob story she ever heard.

But man, did she have a way of making a person feel guilty about not doing the right thing.

Lulu slunk in her chair, running her finger along the rim of her glass. "It's too late."

For once, Viv, who was as daring as Amelia was conservative, agreed with the other woman. "She's right. It's your own fault he's hooking up with a lying ho-bag instead of you." She grinned evilly. "You lying ho-bag."

"Oh, shut up," Lulu snapped, not in the mood for any ribbing.

"This wouldn't have happened if you hadn't played games with him," said Amelia.

"Exactly. None of it would have happened. I wouldn't have had an amazing time with Chaz that almost led to—" She cut herself off before continuing. Lulu hadn't given them all the details of what had happened after she'd left on Halloween night. She might kiss and tell, but she didn't blow and tell.

"Or," Amelia said, presenting an alternate scenario, "maybe if you'd been honest from the start, you two would have had a drink, caught up on old times, danced, and still left together. Only you wouldn't have felt the need to run out on him and pretend you were someone else."

Viv tossed down the rest of her second margarita. "You never did tell us exactly what happened that night. Did you two fuck or not?"

"Viv!" Amelia exclaimed.

"What? It would help in my advice-giving if I knew how far things went."

Lulu just growled.

"Okay, I take it that's a no on the uck-faying?"

Rolling her eyes as she translated Viv's pig Latin attempt at gentility, Lulu replied, "Take it however you want."

Honestly, she wasn't sure how to answer. "Sort of," seemed a little too ambiguous, and she did not want to go into details. How could she explain that she'd had just a taste of him inside her, but the memory of that heated moment was enough to make her shiver with the need to finish what they'd started?

"It's a no," Viv said with a laugh. "You've been acting like a woman who's been put away wet without having been ridden hard."

She could have had somebody ride her hard. Two or three somebodies, probably. She'd certainly had some offers lately, including from a couple of her kickball pals.

But nobody else interested her. Chaz was the only man she wanted…and he was the only man she couldn't have.

Why was that again? Funny, the more wine she sipped, the harder it was to remember.

"I missed my shot," she mumbled, more to herself than to her friends. "He's dating that red-haired girl and doesn't even remember I'm alive."

"Of course he does," said Amelia. "It was obvious the way he came right over to you that night, not even knowing who you were. There was instant chemistry. Out of the whole, crowded club, he zeroed in on you and never even glanced at anyone else."

That made her feel a little better, because it was true. She hadn't tricked him into approaching her, he'd been the aggressor. He'd truly wanted her.

"Just seduce him and he'll forget all about the bitch," said Viv. "I can teach you a few moves. I'm telling you, lick a guy's balls and he's yours forever."

Screeching, Amelia threw her hands over her ears, but Lulu snorted a laugh, inhaling some wine, then coughing it back up. Viv was over-the-top, but she was certainly always good for a laugh.

"Ignore her," said Amelia. "You don't have to play tricks, or, ahem, do anything gross."

Well, having tasted him, Lulu didn't agree that Viv's suggestion was gross. In fact, exploring his entire body with her mouth sounded like pure heaven. But sweet Amelia didn't need to know that.

"Just be honest. Go up to him and tell him the whole story. The truth and nothing but the truth. You can do it!"

Yes, she could admit she'd been sneaky and manipulative, and that she'd lied by omission on Halloween.

And Chaz would hate her for it. He had put up with a lot as a kid, but he'd never put up with anybody lying. It was his personal line in the sand, one he wouldn't cross and wouldn't forgive in someone else. Now, from a few things he'd said to her, she suspected it was an even bigger issue for him.

Damn it, she had left before things went past the point of no return on Halloween because she didn't *want* to lie to Chaz. She hadn't wanted to take advantage of his own male weakness and use him for great, amazing, world-shattering sex without ever revealing who she really was.

So now this Heather chick was probably using him for great, amazing, world-shattering sex without ever revealing who she really *wasn't*. Namely, Lulu!

It just wasn't fair.

"You know, Lulu," said Amelia, sounding cautious, as though she wasn't sure her comment would be welcome, "you haven't mentioned anything about this being just a fling, like you planned when you were going after Schaefer. Is that still all you want, even with Chaz?"

She stared, unsure how to answer. Yes, on Halloween, she'd been after only a brief, sexual adventure. Now, though, especially having spent the past several weeks getting to know Chaz all over again, she feared she wouldn't be content with that. But was she really ready to try for something real, something honest, that went beyond sex? It wasn't just an issue of Chaz wanting to; she, herself, had to be sure she was ready to trust someone.

You can trust Chaz. You know you can.

With her life, maybe. He'd never physically hurt her, or allow anyone else to. But with her heart? Well, that was a whole other story. His career meant everything to him; she'd only ever be a distant second in terms of importance. She might give him her heart, but he'd never completely give her his.

"I don't know," she admitted. "We're friends, we share

a lot, and he'd never make me feel used or unimportant. But I'm just starting a job here that means a lot to me, and he's never in one place for long. That wouldn't make it easy to build something."

"You deserve someone who knows how you're feeling, knows what your dreams are, what you care about, and who you really are," said Amelia, her eyes misty, as if her heart hurt for Lulu.

"Maybe," she said, thinking about it.

"And if that's Chaz, you've got to wrap your mind around the idea that you have to take some risks," Viv said. "Starting with telling him who you were on Halloween night."

Crap. Back to that again. "He'll be so mad. I've lied, and Chaz always hated liars."

"If you tell him before he finds out some other way, at least he'll appreciate you trying to do the right thing," said Amelia.

"I'll just look desperate, like I'm trying to ruin his new romance with what's-her-face."

"Do you know how far it's gotten?" asked Amelia. "Are they, um…serious?"

"Has he made love to her?" asked Viv.

Lulu frowned at her friend. "Oh, very nice. You ask if he's fucked me but if he's made love to her?"

"I was trying to be ladylike and stuff." Viv waved a hand toward Amelia. "I figure I've burned her ears enough for one night. But if you want to be blunt about it…has he banged her or not?"

"They've gone out the past two weekends." She nibbled her lip. "What do you suppose that means?"

"He didn't seem to be a slow mover on Halloween," said Viv.

Lulu had been trying not to think about that. She

glared at the brunette, who immediately back-pedaled. "Of course, that doesn't mean he's as attracted to her as he was to you. There were some serious pheromones that night. You two might as well have started dry-humping in the middle of your dance."

"Thanks. I guess."

"He really seemed crazy about you," said Amelia, nodding loyally. "For all we know, he's gone out with her a few times specifically because he's trying to figure out why he's *not* feeling that same immediate attraction he felt for you. I mean her. Oh, heck, I have no idea what I mean."

"I understood you the first time," Lulu said. "Do you really think it's possible?"

"Definitely," said Amelia.

Viv merely shrugged and sipped her margarita. "Anything's possible." But she didn't sound very convinced.

Lulu wanted to believe Amelia was right, but Chaz *hadn't* been a slow mover, at least not on Halloween. She'd primed him, gotten him totally worked up and ready, and some other woman had moved in for the kill, taking orgasms that should rightfully have been Lulu's.

Orgasms, and now her holiday dinner, too.

"I still can't believe he invited her for Thanksgiving."

Lulu was kicking herself for having agreed to attend. She wouldn't have if she'd known he was going to invite the redhead, who, upon hearing about the pot-luck holiday meal, had claimed she, too, was being "orphaned" by vacationing family members on Thanksgiving. It sounded to Lulu like the schemer had angled for an invitation the way a pro fisherman went after the biggest carp. And Chaz had acted like a well-hooked fish.

Since all their parents were going to be away, Chaz had decided to step up and host a holiday meal for all his friends who had no place else to go. That included her and

Lawrence, Chaz and his sister Sarah, as well as Peggy, Marcia and Frankie.

And Heather. Blech. Stupid secret-identity-stealing Heather.

Good grief, she was the *last* person Lulu wanted to spend a holiday with. If it weren't for the real possibility that World War Three would break out between Sarah and Lawrence, with pumpkin pies and green bean casserole flying, she'd blow off the whole meal.

But she couldn't. She'd told Chaz she would come, and that she'd help him mediate between their younger siblings. She intended to keep her word, even if it meant smiling across the table at the woman who'd stepped in and taken advantage of the man Lulu had gotten all heated up on Halloween. She wouldn't let on what she was really thinking if it killed her.

She kept reminding herself of that a few days later, on the actual holiday.

She'd arrived at Chaz's place early, having promised to help him decipher the instructions on cooking a twenty-pound turkey. As they'd feared, there were innards to deal with, but fortunately they were bagged, and even more fortunately, Chaz was the one who dug them out.

If she hadn't known that Heather would be arriving later in the day, along with the other, more welcome guests, she might have actually enjoyed the time she spent in the kitchen with Chaz. His house was roomy and nicely furnished, and his kitchen pretty well stocked for a bachelor. Lulu wasn't much of a cook, but she'd paid attention when her mom cooked holiday meals and certainly felt capable of sugaring a few yams and mashing some potatoes. Anything she didn't remember how to do, Chaz was quick to figure out, or look up on the internet.

They made a pretty good team, if she did say so herself.

Since that day a couple of weeks ago, when they'd kissed, he'd gone back to treating her like a friend from back home. There'd been no flirtation. He'd been just a little overprotective but hadn't pried too much into her business. He sure hadn't kissed her, though she had turned around once or twice and caught him looking at her with an intensity he usually kept hidden.

It was at those moments she was sure he hadn't forgotten their kiss any more than she had.

They'd opened Pandora's box. They both knew how good they could be together, and it was impossible to un-remember that delicious, intense passion. They might have shoved it back in the box and vowed to never take it out again, but that didn't mean they didn't both think about it and wonder. And wonder. And wonder.

Usually, though, they managed to behave like nothing had happened. They still walked together to the train every day, still socialized with others on weekends. Lawrence had come over a few times. He and Chaz had become close again, as they'd been when they were kids, when Chaz had served as a big brother figure, before Sarah had come between them.

She and Chaz had so much in common, so much shared history, and truly enjoyed each other's company now. Today had been laid-back and easy, fun and a little silly. He'd teased her about taking as much potato as peel, she'd harassed him for not knowing you had to add sugar to fresh cranberries to make a sauce. They drank a little wine, occasionally exchanging a long, studied glance when their hands brushed over a towel or their legs made contact under the table. The rivalry and tension from their childhood was gone, the awareness warm and unthreatening, and they got along so well it was almost as though they were a couple.

At least, until the doorbell rang.

Heather, who'd called out, "Yoo-hoo," as she passed by the kitchen window, was out front. Heather with the perfect smile and the cutest little upturned nose matched by what Lulu suspected were surgically enhanced upturned tits. Heather who was occupying a place in Chaz's life, in his memories, maybe even in his bed, that rightfully belonged to Lulu.

Chaz was basting the bird and asked her to get the door. Drying her hands on a dish towel, which she whipped over her shoulder, she strode out of the kitchen and yanked open the front door.

"Hello, Heather," she said as she ushered the other woman in. "You're early. Nobody else is here yet."

Heather's smile was small and tight. She'd obviously expected someone else to answer the door. Someone far more susceptible to red hair, a phony smile and equally phony tits.

"Hello, Lulu. I thought I'd come early in case Chaz needed any help."

"I think we have everything under control."

The redhead shoved a foil-wrapped, pie-shaped object into Lulu's waiting hands. "Well, I'll just cheer you two on then, shall I? But first I have to freshen up."

"Whatever," she mumbled, turning and heading for the kitchen. She didn't wait to see if Heather followed or made herself at home, because, frankly, she didn't want the proof that the other women had been here enough to know her way around.

The two women had met that day at the bar, when Chaz had first spotted Heather and made such a fool of himself trying to find out if she recognized him from a former meeting. Like from having given him a blowjob in an ATM vestibule.

The devious woman had played it smart. Being pursued by a gorgeous, successful, charming man, she hadn't immediately denied being the Halloween witch he sought, nor had she confirmed it. She just acted mysterious and coy, and what American man didn't go ape over those kinds of women? She'd played him better than Schaefer played his guitar, and Chaz was too fascinated to notice.

It had been all Lulu could do to not out her for a phony right then and there. Of course, the only way she could have done that would have been to out herself, as well. And that she was not ready to do.

"She brought pie," Lulu said as she entered the kitchen, putting the dessert on the counter. Chaz didn't even look up, busy trying to figure out how to cut into a big, softball-size vegetable. "You'd better be careful, you might lose a finger cutting into that Winnebago."

"It's a rutabaga. I can't believe you don't remember my mom making these every Christmas."

"Guess I always snuck it onto Lawrence's plate when nobody was looking."

"Where is Heather?" he asked, still gazing only at the waxy vegetable and the big-ass knife in his hand. He didn't sound terribly excited about the arrival, and didn't dash off to kiss her passionately in welcome, which made Lulu feel a little better.

"Being nosy and checking the balance in your checkbook, I think."

He lifted a brow at her tone.

"She's in the bathroom," she admitted. "Freshening up her face for you."

"You don't like her, huh?"

"I don't know her enough to like her or dislike her." Licking her lips and pretending to be entirely focused on a recipe for green bean casserole, which she could probably make blindfolded, she asked, "Do *you* like her?"

He thought about it, a confused expression on his face. "Honestly, I'm not sure. Sometimes I think I do. Other times I wonder what on earth it was about her that so fascinated me the night we met."

Lulu's teeth slammed together and she clenched them tightly. She had to pry her words out from between them with brute force. "So, you'd met her before that day we played kickball?"

You idiot, are you totally blind? How dare you think she's me? There's not one real, natural thing about her!

He lowered the big knife he'd been using, glanced toward the doorway, and lowered his voice to say, "I don't know. I thought so, but I'm just not sure. She seems…different than the woman I met, the one I've been looking for. And she's so mysterious about it, she won't confirm or deny anything when I ask her about it."

Lulu swallowed, hard. "This woman you met, the one you're looking for? What was so special about her?"

Chaz shook his head slowly, visibly lost in thought. "I honestly don't know that, either. I'm not even sure the damn night actually happened. Maybe I was so jet-lagged I crashed when I got home from my trip and dreamed up some elaborate fantasy."

She gulped. She didn't want him thinking Heather was the woman he'd been with…but was him convincing himself it hadn't really happened any better?

Well, yeah, if she wanted to keep her secret, it probably was. But part of her wasn't sure about that secret anymore. Okay, so they weren't going to let anything happen between them…would it be the crime of the century if he found out she was the one he'd come so close to hooking up with that night? At least he'd know the truth and wouldn't be driving himself crazy trying to imprint his memories of that night onto the face of someone who didn't even have the guts to tell him he had the wrong girl.

"Well hey there, happy Thanksgiving!"

Heather walked into the kitchen. She'd taken off her jacket. She'd also obviously spent time in front of the bathroom mirror, fluffing up her windblown hair to make it look more artfully windblown. She'd smeared bright red lipstick across her lips, and pulled her sweater down to reveal more of the silicone.

Ignoring Lulu, she walked around to the other side of the kitchen island and lifted her face, pursing her lips for a kiss. Chaz, Lulu noted, hesitated, glancing in her direction before obliging his date. If she had to guess, she'd say he was a little uncomfortable.

Good. Because if he couldn't tell that woman's kiss from hers, he deserved what he got.

"I'm going to double-check the Ping-Pong table," Lulu said, trying to keep the disgust out of her voice. If she had to see Chaz kiss another woman, she might just be the one flinging the pie and green bean casserole.

"Isn't there a lot to still do?" Heather asked, pretending she didn't care that she hadn't gotten her kiss.

But Lulu cared. Oh, hell, yes, she did. She hid her smile, though, not wanting Chaz to notice and interpret it. "Yes, quite a lot," she said.

"If you want to play a game, Lulu, don't worry about it. I'll fill in here."

Lulu smirked. "Uh, the Ping-Pong table is the only thing Chaz had that was big enough to seat everybody around. We're eating on it down in the rec room."

The woman's eyes rounded and her smile faded a tiny bit. Perhaps she was picturing a fancy holiday meal from an internationally published journalist. But she wasn't going to get it.

Frankly, Lulu loved the effort Chaz had gone to for them. Her heart had melted a little bit when she'd arrived and seen him putting a pristine white tablecloth over the huge table, setting it with new dishes he'd picked up just for today. He'd shoved a bunch of mismatched chairs, including outdoor ones, around the table, determined to make it a great holiday, not just for his friends, but also for his bratty little sister, spending her first holiday away from home.

How many guys would go to so much trouble? Not many, she knew. That was just one thing that made Chaz so special.

If Heather didn't see and appreciate that, she didn't deserve him. Hell, she didn't deserve him period!

And somehow, no matter what it cost her personally, Lulu hoped Chaz found out the truth about the other woman, and realized she was not worth his time and trouble. He deserved better.

ALTHOUGH CHAZ HAD worried a lot about the presence of both Sarah and Lawrence at today's holiday dinner, his sister and Lulu's brother managed to surprise him. They'd apparently seen each other on campus and now were both perfectly cordial, if not exactly warm. The younger pair had finally grown up. So in that respect, things were going great.

The problem had come from an entirely different direction. Chaz found his peace of mind most disturbed by having both Heather and Lulu here.

It was crazy. He and Lulu were old friends; they'd both agreed that's what they would remain. End of story. And Heather was a woman he'd just started dating who was new to town and had nowhere else to go. It had seemed perfectly natural for them both to be invited. But now that they were both here, sitting at opposite ends of the Ping-Pong table ignoring each other easily in this big group, he couldn't help comparing them—and realizing he'd made a mistake. Possibly a big one.

Heather *might* be the woman whose memory had tantalized and tormented him for weeks. She *might* be the one who had flooded him with want and erotic fantasy.

But she sure didn't feel like it.

They'd gone out twice before today, and while he thought she was attractive, he hadn't experienced that out-of-breath, heart-pounding, palm-sweating, pant-tenting excitement, not even when they'd kissed. Nor had his usually subtle, but sometimes direct questions about whether she was the one he'd met on Halloween night yielded any definite answers. She hadn't said yes. She hadn't said no. She'd hinted and hemmed and hawed. His sexy witch had hidden her name from him on Halloween night, so she obviously did like being mysterious. But he'd never felt like she was playing games. He wasn't so sure about Heather, who, he suspected, could be a game-player. The only thing he knew for sure was that he felt not only confused but untouched.

Nothing about Heather touched him at his most basic, elemental level, the way it had on Halloween.

He'd invited her for Thanksgiving before he'd come to the realization that she was probably not his mystery/fantasy woman. But since he was no closer to finding that woman, and since Heather was attractive and interested, he had decided to play this out with her.

All that had seemed smart.

Until he'd spent much of the day with Lulu.

Lulu was a brat from his past, the girl next door, the little witch who'd busted his ass, literally.

She was not supposed to feel so natural by his side. She

was not supposed to inspire thoughts of hot kisses and sweaty sheets. Her hair wasn't supposed to feel so soft and sensuous against his skin. The sight of her hands shouldn't make parts of his body tense in anticipation of her touch.

What the hell was happening here?

"I still can't believe the parents all went on a cruise for Thanksgiving. But I have to say, you did a really good job today, big brother."

Chaz tore his mind off the confusing women in his life—*woman, one, Lulu is not in your life, not as a woman anyway*—and smiled at his kid sister.

"Thanks. I couldn't have done it without Lulu."

"Well, thanks to you, too, Lulu," Sarah said, sounding sincere and being nice to Lulu, with whom there was usually tension. Then she ruined it by smirking. "I guess we should all just be glad you both survived it. With the track record between you, and all those sharp objects in the kitchen, it's lucky nobody was scarred or maimed."

Lulu picked up her wine glass, bringing it to her lips. "The night's still young," she mumbled before sipping.

"Were these two really nemeses like we've heard?" asked Peggy, who was rubbing her full stomach with one hand, while patting Marcia's with another.

Lulu's kid brother, Lawrence, who looked as a young man exactly as he had when a young boy—a little small, angular face, deep, soulful eyes, and kind smile—answered. "Only because they were in love with each other."

Chaz dropped his fork. It landed with a clatter on his plate. But even that wasn't loud enough to cover Lulu's immediate exclamation.

"That is crazy!"

She sounded like somebody had just accused her of robbing a church, which wasn't exactly flattering.

Of course, his vehemence probably didn't make her

feel any better when he snapped, "I doubt Lulu was in love with me when she cut off all my hair with her Fiskar scissors during recess."

"It grew back," she sniped. "And I doubt you were in love with me when you told all your friends that I wet the bed."

"You did."

"When I was three!"

"Nobody ever asked for clarification," he said, his smile taunting. "I never lied."

"No, you never do, Saint Chaz."

"Whoa, whoa, sorry," said Peggy, holding up her hands, palm out, to each of them, acting as referee. "I didn't mean to start a war here."

"Wow, it sounds to me like you two can't stand each other," said Heather, whose sweet smile didn't quite hide the gleam of happiness in her eye. He had to wonder if the redhead had picked up on some of the vibes between him and Lulu.

"Okay, subject change," said Marcia as she licked the last of her mashed potatoes off her fork. "Lulu, I've been meaning to ask you, how's work going? Has our donation been distributed yet?"

"Donation?" Heather asked.

Chaz listened, too. Lulu had never really talked about her job, and he honestly didn't know what she did, beyond working in an office up on Massachusetts Avenue. Her master's degree was in political science, so he assumed she was doing something connected with one of the many embassies up in that part of the city.

"Yes, it has," Lulu said, smiling at Marcia.

"Do you know who it went to?"

"Several women from one family in a village in Tanzania formed a farming co-op, and that's where your donation went." Her posture relaxed and passion came through in her voice. "I am sure you'll be getting a letter from them. All of the participants in the program are so incredibly appreciative."

"What is it you do exactly?" asked Heather, sounding merely polite rather than truly interested.

"Oh, Lulu works for a great organization that puts microloans in the hands of mothers in third-world countries so they can start businesses to support their families," said Peggy. "What's it called again, Lulu?"

"Hands Across The Waters," Lulu said.

Chaz frowned. The name sounded familiar, and it wasn't just because it was from a Beatles song.

Then it clicked. He'd recently been talking to his friend Tonia about that very same organization. She'd mentioned an investigation she was working on that day when they'd played kickball up at the Mall.

He'd been excited to hear about her work because he wanted to pump her for more information in the hopes that he could find his mystery woman from Halloween. Of course, that very same afternoon, he'd met Heather, and had forgotten all about it.

His heart beat a little faster in his chest. An errant thought whizzed through his mind, as quick and directionless as a fly whizzing by. Something insubstantial, something impossible, something that couldn't even fully take shape as an idea in his brain.

He lifted his water glass and sipped from it, unable to take his eyes off Lulu's face. She was happy now, animated when discussing something she obviously cared deeply about. Her dark eyes sparkled, her smile was quick and easy. Her soft, dark hair framed her creamy-skinned face, the thick strands caught in a clip at the base of her neck.

Damn, she was beautiful. Exciting, charming, daring, sexy.

So sexy. So intriguing.

Oh, Jesus.

No. It wasn't possible. That whizzing thought tried to form a picture in his mind, attempted to present an absurd possibility. Chaz just wouldn't allow it. He *couldn't*.

Still, something made his lips form words, and he said, "So, Peggy, you asked if Lulu and I were always nemeses. Did she tell you about the time she swiped all the candy bars out of my trick-or-treat bag and replaced them with raisins?" He caught Lulu's stare, unblinking, cautious, and added, "She was dressed as a *witch* that year, I think. Appropriate, don't you agree?"

Lulu's tiny gasp might have been overlooked by everyone at the table. Everyone but Chaz.

Her dark eyes went as round as silver dollars and color flooded her cheeks. Her lush lips trembled, and her fingers clenched reflexively on the table, squeezing the white tablecloth into her fists.

Son of a bitch.

The truth began to assert itself in his mind. Wheels turned, cogs clicked, and the whole picture assembled, moment by moment, of that strange Halloween night.

It had been her. Lulu had been the mysterious witch.

She'd been the woman haunting his dreams, the woman with whom he'd shared some of the most wild, uninhibited moments of his life. Lulu.

Marcia smiled broadly, completely oblivious, as was everyone else at the table, to the rising tension between Chaz and Lulu. "That's funny. Lulu was a witch this year, too."

"Was she really?" he murmured, his voice low, his eyes glued to Lulu's stricken face. "Was she a scary witch with an ugly wig and mask?"

"Oh, no. She looked so hot in her black leather bustier, with her hair dyed red, and a green Mardi Gras mask, I thought for sure a bunch of guys would follow her home and camp out in front of our building to get a chance with her."

"I can imagine," he said, sounding so calm, so reasonable, nobody else might have even realized that inside he was a seething mask of emotion. Humiliation warred with shock, but anger trumped all.

Lulu was the only one who understood. She had to have seen something in him—a spark of fury he couldn't hide—for she suddenly slapped her hands on the table and launched herself from her seat. Everyone gaped at her, but she didn't look around. She remained focused only on Chaz. All the color that had been rising in her cheeks fell out and she went as white as the sheet he'd worn when masquerading as a ghost.

"I'm sorry, I'm suddenly not feeling well," she said, her voice shaking. She brought a melodramatic hand to her face and covered her mouth. "I have to go."

The others all expressed concern and asked if she needed help, but Lulu had already spun on her heel and raced for the stairs, thumping up them two at a time in her hurry to get away.

Chaz didn't race. He didn't chase her. He didn't yell or hunt her down or demand answers or embarrass her or cause a scene.

He knew where she was going. He knew exactly where to find her.

If she thought her locked apartment door was going to keep him out, she was wrong.

If she thought she could get away with acting as though she hadn't made an utter fool out of him for the past month, she was crazy.

If she thought he wouldn't mind that she'd been lying to him for weeks, she was deluded.

And if she thought he was just going to forget what had happened between them, forget the incredible night they'd almost shared, she was out of her God-damned mind.

9

LULU WAS NO COWARD, but as soon as she got back to her apartment, she locked the door, ran into her room, dove into her bed and pulled the covers up over her head.

"He knows," she whispered, horrifying herself by saying the words out loud.

Chaz had figured it out. She had been so stupid, gushing on about her work. But Marcia had asked her directly, and she'd gotten carried away by the love she had for what she did.

When everything came crashing down around her at the dinner table, she'd half expected him to erupt right there. Steam had practically risen off his head. She honestly couldn't ever remember seeing him so intense as he'd been today. She wasn't sure she could even describe what she saw—rage? Shock? Humiliation? Yes, probably all of the above. Enough to chase her out of there, as if a swarm of wasps was on her tail.

But she'd also detected something else in his eyes— sheer determination. As if he were really looking forward to whatever came next. She just didn't know whether he was picturing something good—like them finally finishing what they'd started; or something bad—like him telling her exactly how much he hated her.

Or worse.

Undoubtedly, Chaz had been furious at having been made a fool of, and probably wouldn't believe her when she told him that hadn't been her intention. With all the dark water under the bridge of their relationship, he might believe the whole thing had been a scheme. He might smell a setup, figuring she'd decided to make him look and feel stupid for not recognizing her.

He was wrong, of course. If anything, she was the one who looked and felt stupid for playing these games…and then getting caught.

But that anticipation could be about something else entirely. And it was the something else that had her literally shaking, every cell in her body awake and sparking with life.

Throughout the evening, she kept watching the clock, flinching at every noise from outside. She felt the way she had when she was a kid and she'd done something bad, and her mother had sent her to her room with the standard, "Just you wait until your father comes home!" warning.

She was on edge, tense, wondering what her punishment would be, listening for that deep voice, or that heavy foot in the hallway. She heard the couple downstairs come in, him yelling about something, her shushing him. When Marcia and Peggy got home and softly knocked on her door to check on her, she remained quiet, wanting them to assume she was in bed.

Nine o'clock swept past. Then ten.

By ten-thirty, she was beginning to think he wasn't coming, and she couldn't decide whether she was relieved or disappointed.

Maybe he was so angry, he couldn't stand to face her yet, wanting to calm down and talk to her tomorrow.

Or perhaps he was so disgusted at wasting a month lusting after *her* that he'd leapt right into bed with Heather, to wash the bad memories out of his mind.

"I'll kill him," she muttered, torturing herself with the mental picture of it.

Ten forty-five.

She glared toward his house through her window, seeing all the lights were off. Had he just gone to sleep, not even thinking about her at all?

Tense, angry, scared, worried, she tore her clothes off and put on a pair of pajamas, prepared for a long night of restless discomfort. But she couldn't go to bed yet. Pacing her small apartment, she considered getting re-dressed and going down to his place. If she and Chaz were going to have it out, she wanted it over with. The tension—the waiting—was killing her.

The knock came at eleven-oh-five.

It was sharp, perfunctory. Two hard raps, then silence.

She ran to the door, her heart in her mouth, her stomach churning with real anxiety now. As she unfastened the lock, she formed explanations and apologies, trying to guess what kind of mood he would be in and how best to handle it.

She was prepared for frustrated Chaz. Or for sad Chaz. Or for confused Chaz.

What she got was wildly sexy Chaz.

The minute she pulled the door open, he pushed his way in and then kicked it closed behind him. He raked a hot, thorough stare over her, taking in the scooped neckline of her silky pajama top, and the flimsy shorts that left her bare from the top of her thighs down to the tips of her toes.

"Chaz, I…"

"To use your favorite expression, just shut up, Lulu."

Then he grabbed her in his arms and pulled her to him, burying one hand in her hair and twisting tightly. He gripped her ass, hoisting her up until the juncture of her thighs met the thickness straining against his zipper. She was groaning with need when he covered her mouth with his, plunging his tongue deep.

He kissed her as if he'd invented kissing. Exploring every corner, every crevice, he licked into her as if he were starving and she his only means of survival.

Strength deserted her. She sagged into him, her legs turning to jelly, her arms too weak to do any more than rest across his strong shoulders.

This was a Chaz she'd never seen before in her life, one she didn't even recognize.

And he excited her beyond all measure.

He scooped her up, swinging her into his arms and striding across the small apartment toward her bedroom. When he reached the bed, he tossed her down on it and followed her. He was heavy, crushing, but she welcomed his weight, wanting his frenzy, needing every bit of his untamed passion.

"Wait," she breathed. "Heather?"

"Gone. For good."

Oh, thank heaven.

He kissed her, and the kiss went on and on. He swallowed her every exhalation, sucking away any possible rejection, his tongue plunging, lapping, devouring. He didn't give her a second to think or consider, making her exist only in this moment of heat and wild desire.

When he drew back to pull in a raspy breath, she reached up to cup his cheek. He ducked away, not in the mood for tenderness, not even in the mood for her to say yes or to welcome him.

He wanted her. He'd wanted her for weeks, after she'd led him on and brought him to a fever pitch of desire. She'd made a fool of him, knowing all along that she was who he sought, and now he was going to have his due.

There would be no turning back tonight. He wouldn't allow it.

She knew Chaz. She trusted him. She had no doubt he would never hurt her. But in this mood, he wasn't going to give her the chance to say a single word, especially if that word was *no*.

She wouldn't have said it—the word didn't even exist in her vocabulary right now. He was making her insane with want, driving her so high, making her quake and writhe on the bed, wanting his mouth and his hands everywhere. How could she possibly form the word *no* when every molecule in her body screamed *yes,* and *yes,* and *yes!*

Lulu reached up to unbutton her top, but he shoved her hands away and caught the fabric in his own. He wrenched the two sides apart, sending buttons flying, baring her to her waist.

Eyeing her hungrily, he fell on her, sucking her puckered nipple into his mouth, drawing hard. Such pleasure, the tiniest hint of pain that only made it that much better.

He went to her other breast—equal time—suckling her, squeezing her, pinching ever so lightly. She felt each sensation down low in her groin, moisture flooding her, the folds of her sex swelling.

He kept going, down, down her body, nipping, licking. When she moved too much, or begged silently with an upward thrust, he put his hands on her hips, holding tight, and pushed her hard against the bed.

He was so strong, his big hands holding her immobile. He would do what he wanted, and the message was clear— she was going to lie there and take it.

Heavens, what woman in her right mind would even consider doing anything else?

Down farther as he tore her silky shorts off. No part of her was left unexplored—his tongue in her belly button, his teeth on her hipbone, and finally, his hot breaths parting the curls at the apex of her thighs. Farther, and now he licked into her most delicate folds, finding unerringly the spot on her body where all sensation centered and seethed.

"Oh, God, yes," she cried when he covered her clit and pleasured her thoroughly.

He didn't stay still. Moving farther down, he buried his face between her legs, looping one leg over his shoulder, opening her fully. She had no secrets, no dignity, could hold absolutely nothing back. And she truly didn't care.

Chaz explored her, inhaling deeply as if he needed to breathe her scent into his lungs and lock it there forever. His lips sank into her, finding her opening, pushing inside, invading her, devouring her. He made love to her with his tongue, slow laps deep within her, mimicking what he would do with his fingers, with his cock.

She began to softly groan, breaking the silence with helpless sobs of pleasure. Tossing her head back and forth on the pillow, she reached for something that was just out of her grasp. The tension was almost painful, the pleasure beyond anything in this world.

He seemed to take pity, as if aware he had to give her something so she could keep going. Moving back to her clit, he scooped all around the base of it with his tongue, gliding, flicking, sucking, until hot bolts of pulsating heat flooded her. She came hard in his mouth, and he lapped at her, taking everything her body threw at him and savoring it.

Lulu was barely even conscious of him standing up beside the bed to pull his shirt off. He tossed it to the floor before unfastening his belt. Unbuttoning and unzipping his pants, he reached in and pulled out that enormous, hard cock. She stared at it, wanting him so badly, knowing she'd die if he wasn't in her soon.

He dropped onto on his knees on the bed, staring down at her, wrapping one hand around his erection and lazily stroking. He was pleasuring himself. Teasing her. Building her hunger.

God, it worked. She wanted him with a desperation bordering on insanity.

"Please, Chaz,"

"Hush," he ordered.

"I need you to…"

"I mean it, Lulu. Not a word."

"But…"

He glared at her. "I waited for hours to calm down, and then came over here, knowing I'd have to either drag you over my knee and spank your gorgeous ass, or kiss you into silence until I was calm enough to talk to you. Say another word and I won't be responsible for which way this goes."

She licked her lips, more turned on than ever by his words and his no-nonsense tone. Lulu had never seen him like this, never even imagined he could be so sexually aggressive. But she knew he meant it. And part of her wanted him to make good on his threat.

She'd never dreamed that fantasy would appeal to her, but she knew Chaz, she trusted him completely. If he put her over his knee and spanked her, she was certain each stinging slap would be followed by a caress.

After the punishment, he would have her lie face down on the bed while he kissed away the pain. She could see it, the fantasy unrolling in her mind.

Then, perhaps, they would both be so aroused by his attention to her bare bottom—which would be thrust up to him in utter invitation—that he'd take her like that, invade her where no one ever had before, introducing her to something new and dark and erotic.

And she wanted it. She wanted all of it. Wanted him to take her in every way a woman could be taken, wanted to give all that she had to give.

Someday. Oh, yes, someday, she would make that kinky fantasy come true. He was the one man she trusted to give her that kind of dangerous, edgy pleasure.

But for right now, she just wanted him to bury himself in her pussy. She'd been tormented by the memories of that tiny little taste of bliss he'd given her outside on Halloween night, and her insides were crying for the full connection.

Chaz had been watching her, as if reading her thoughts, knowing where her imagination was taking her.

She swallowed, but didn't say a word, merely offering him the kind of smile that said she understood what he'd thought about doing to her…and would someday let him do it.

"You drive me insane," he muttered, looking driven past the edge of endurance. "Are you on birth control?"

Remembering not to speak out loud, she simply nodded.

"Good. Hold on."

She reached up and held on, digging her nails into his shoulders. Chaz moved between her parted thighs. He wasn't tender, he wasn't cautious. He'd made her dripping wet and he knew it. So he pushed his cock between the lips of her sex, found her opening, and plunged deep, tearing her apart in the most delicious, most satisfying way.

Gasping, she arched into him, taking him all the way. She hadn't had sex in a long time, and never with someone of such generous proportions. He filled her to her core, and she savored every inch of him.

Dropping down to catch her mouth in another deep, devouring kiss, he began to ease out of her, and then thrust back. His movements were so deliberate and determined, slightly wild. But she still never feared he would hurt her. He was incapable of that.

Instinct took over and she caught his rhythm and matched it. She rose up for every downward thrust, squeezing him deep inside. He might be in the driver's seat, but she felt the shudders of his lean, strong body and knew he was every bit as affected. He was losing himself to this, unable to remain controlled when wracked with such intense sensations.

They never slowed down, twisting and pounding, giving and taking. As if wanting to go as deep as humanly possible, Chaz hooked his arms around her legs and lifted them both over his shoulders. She let out a little scream of pleasure as he gained even more of her. He kissed away her cries of pleasure, driving mindlessly. The position was shockingly fulfilling, and gave her just enough pressure against her clit that she spilled into another climax, throbbing with it. Her obvious passion pushed him past all limits. With one more deep thrust, he threw his head back, his muscles tightening, every inch of him straining, and shuddered as he came deep inside her. Lulu squeezed him, sucking him dry of every drop, clinging to him with arms, legs and body.

Afterward, he collapsed, but even in his exhaustion, he didn't let all his weight fall on her, protective as always. He remained inside her, but moved onto his side, pulling her with him, their legs tangled, her hair still wrapped in his hands.

One more kiss—this one softer, more tender. She returned it with heartfelt emotion, wondering if he had spent all his anger and would now forgive her for her deceit. Or if he'd just gotten started and would now commence with the lecture.

She opened her mouth to ask, but he narrowed his eyes and shook his head.

"Sleep, Lulu. We'll talk tomorrow."

He had offered her a reprieve. A night wrapped in his arms sounded much better than a lot of arguing, and she almost thanked him, but figured she'd better keep her mouth shut. So she merely nodded lazily, smiling, happy and utterly content. Not really caring about what discomfort the morning would bring, she curled even closer, closed her eyes, and drifted to sleep.

WHAT ON EARTH had he done? Twice?

Chaz wondered that as he woke, slowly pulling himself from a wet dream that proved to be reality, since he was still entwined with Lulu, his half-erect dick still inside her. They were wrapped together, limbs, hands, hair, everything, as if neither of them had been able to stand to pull apart while they slept.

Morning light was sifting in through the shades, but it was soft and new. He guessed it was no later than seven. He'd slept soundly for a few hours, after waking up during the night to make silent, erotic love to her again. Neither of them had said a word; they'd simply let their bodies do the talking. He'd held her hips as she climbed on top of him, riding him hard, her fingers digging into his chest, while his hands entwined in her dark hair and toyed with those incredibly sensitive breasts. By the time he was nearing his climax, he was gripping her hips, guiding her, pulling her down onto him with forceful grunts until they'd both cried out their pleasure and she'd collapsed on top of him.

God, he was hard again just thinking about it.

Lulu noticed. She didn't say anything, didn't even open

her eyes. She merely parted her legs and pulled him over onto her. Chaz let himself be pulled, sinking deeply into her wet heat. She fit him like a glove, all soft and welcoming. He'd never felt this kind of life-altering pleasure before. Chaz enjoyed sex, a lot, but had never been driven into an almost animal frenzy, as if he had to mate or die, before last night.

He could become addicted to this.

He cupped her face in his hand, rubbing his thumb across her swollen lips. Her dark eyes drifted open and she smiled up at him. "Good morning," she whispered. Then she sucked her lips into her mouth, her eyes widening as her body tensed.

She'd just remembered he hadn't allowed her to speak last night. He would bet she hadn't been truly afraid of him, knowing he would never really do her harm, but her expression was cautious, worried.

She had reason to worry. He was still bloody furious with her.

But he also wanted to make slow, sweet love to her. So his righteous anger was just going to have to wait a little while.

"Good morning," he whispered, still wondering what had come over him last night. He'd never been so forceful with a woman, never been so torn between desire and anger. Finally they'd swirled together, combining to urge him into the kind of wild sex he'd never had with anyone else.

And never would again, he'd venture. Because Lulu was the only woman he'd ever known who could drive him mad with fury one second and utterly desperate with sexual need the next.

She wrapped her arms around his neck, pressing her mouth to his as they moved together. It was lazy and languorous. He groaned with each slow, deep stroke, not desperate to reach a destination this time, just enjoying the journey.

That wasn't all he wanted to enjoy. She had been ready for him the moment she woke up, but he'd missed out on several delicious steps to get her there. So he moved his mouth away from hers, kissing his way down her chin and her neck, burying his face in the hollow and breathing in that unique Lulu scent.

She was soft everywhere, though not weak—he felt the strength of her, especially in those thighs and the arms that had gripped him close throughout the night. But her body was a wonderland of slopes and valleys, all tender, all sensitive, all waiting to be explored.

He moved lower, licking the curve of her breast, tracing the tip of his tongue around her pink nipple.

"Mmm, yes, please," she sighed. Then she added, "I'm allowed to speak now, right?"

"As long as you focus on telling me how to make you feel good."

"You do," she said, running her fingers through his hair, holding him tight to her breast as he began to suckle her. "Oh, *so* good, Chaz."

He wanted to make her feel even better. And he wanted to explore her more slowly this morning, as the early sun bathed her with light, spotlighting all the delicious places he'd almost attacked the night before. He was slow and deliberate, gentle and insistent as he toured her body. He kissed her from her breasts to her belly, her hip, all the way down her leg to the tips of her toes, and then back up the other way. Her skin was velvet smooth, the intoxicating scent of female arousal pouring off her. By the time he got up to the top of her other thigh, she was trembling.

She arched toward him, silently inviting him to do what he most wanted.

He gently parted her thighs, exposing her to his intimate gaze. She was red and swollen, the wild sex of the night before having left its mark. He pressed his mouth to that tender flesh, licking her gently, wanting nothing but to soothe her into a fever pitch.

It was easy, so damned easy. She rocked against his mouth, hissing when he covered her pert clit and stroked it with his tongue.

"Oh, yes, there," she begged, her desire making her sound a little frantic. He had learned so much about what pleased her during the night, and knew exactly what she needed and where she needed it. He caressed her clit, sucking gently until her whole body tightened and then relaxed as her orgasm washed over her. She was already so wet, so juicy, but her climax brought another flood of moisture onto his tongue, and he drank her up, knowing he could swallow nothing but Lulu for the rest of his life and die a well-fed man.

"Come back to me," she urged, reaching for him, tugging at his shoulders.

He couldn't resist her, and slid up again, returning to his place between her parted thighs.

"That mouth of yours is almost as amazing as *this*," she said as she reached down and stroked his cock with the tips of her fingers. "I want to explore you that way, too."

"Later," he told her. "I owed you one, remember?"

She sucked in an audible breath, catching her lip between her teeth. He'd reminded her of that night, the one that had been driving him crazy for weeks. They were both thinking of the way she'd gotten down on her knees and sucked him into insanity.

"Chaz, I..."

"Later," he insisted, tensing. He didn't want to spoil this with conversation right now. He just wanted to lose himself in her, one more time, before he got the answers he'd been seeking.

So he did. He sank into her, into hot, creamy Lulu, feeling her adjust to him, welcome him. She wrapped her legs around his hips, her arms around his shoulders, and pressed close. They rocked together, slow, easy, romantic. And when she came again, climaxing right along with him, she whispered, "God, I'm sorry I wasted a month of our lives not telling you the truth."

He was past replying, falling to the bed, tugging her on top of him and holding her as they drifted back to sleep. But the words echoed, and when he woke up an hour or two later, they were the first thing he thought of.

She was already awake. When he opened his eyes, he found her lying across him, staring at him, her fingers tracing the outline of his lips.

"Good morning again," she said, her voice soft, almost shy.

"What time is it?"

"Around nine. Are you hungry?"

He shook his head.

"Oh." Her face fell. "I had hoped I could make you some waffles."

Waffles. Or pancakes. Or Lucky Charms.

He remembered.

Hell, she was intentionally reminding him.

He stiffened. "Can we do this after I take a shower?"

She played dumb. "Do what?"

"Talk about what a fool you made of me?"

"Oh, no!" Lulu sat up on the bed, the covers falling onto her lap, her beautiful body covered by nothing but her long, thick hair. "That wasn't it at all, Chaz, at least that wasn't my intention."

Realizing he wasn't going to get his shower—and, actually, not wanting it, now that his indignation was on the rise again, he sat up, too.

"What *did* you intend, Lulu?" he asked, remembering that night, wondering how on earth he could have spent such intimate moments with her and not seen the truth of it in her eyes when they'd met next. How had he not recognized that mouth, those soft cheeks, that delicate neck?

He shook his head, needing to focus on the conversation, not on how beautiful she was. Not on what a blind fool he'd been.

"I wanted you, so much," she said, her voice trembling with sincerity.

That tremble got to him, shot right to his heart. She'd opened herself to him fully last night, in every way possible, trusting him, fulfilling him, overwhelming him. He had no doubt she was telling the truth—Lulu wanted him. She had on Halloween night, and she still did.

But he couldn't think about that. He couldn't allow himself to soften by looking at her and remembering every heated thing they'd done together. He needed to get a grip, to take a break, splash some water on his face. Calm his racing mind.

"Give me a minute," he ordered, throwing the sheets back and getting out of bed. Ignoring her tiny sound of protest, he strode toward the bathroom, needing to regroup and prepare for battle.

He came out a few minutes later, having slung a towel around his hips, and found her clad in a short bathrobe, perched on the edge of the bed, as if about to flee.

She didn't know what to expect from him, unable to

gauge his mood. He found he liked having that advantage, and jumped right in. "When did you launch this scheme?"

"It wasn't a scheme, I swear. I assumed you'd recognized me from across the bar. That's why I smiled at you. I just figured you came over and asked me to dance so we could catch up."

"How was I supposed to recognize you when I hadn't seen you for half a decade? When your hair was red, your face was masked, and you looked like a sex goddess and not the girl next door I remembered?"

She clenched her hands in her lap, twisting her fingers in the tie of her robe. "I wasn't thinking clearly. I recognized you, but I was pretty stunned. You… God, Chaz, I was so attracted to you! I couldn't believe it, and certainly didn't want you to realize it. I thought we were playing around and that you knew exactly who I was—at least, right up until you told me your name and asked for mine."

He remembered. That had been while they were dancing. To think, a few misplaced words, a few assumptions, and none of this might have happened. Ever.

That sobered him. If he had recognized her, if she'd called him by name the moment he'd come up to her table, making it clear she knew him, he'd have figured out her identity. And nothing that followed would have happened. Including last night. Last-*amazing*-night.

He couldn't let that sway him, though. The ends didn't justify the means. The life-altering sex didn't excuse the lie.

"Once you realized I didn't know who you were, why didn't you say something?"

"At first, I thought it was kind of funny, I wanted to tease you."

"It worked. You teased me. For a damn month." He swept a hand through his hair, stalking back and forth across the room. "Why the hell did you let things go so far? What we did in that bank vestibule..."

"Was incredible," she whispered. "I loved every second of it."

So had he. That wasn't the point. "And then?"

"I intended to go home with you, but every step we took reminded me that sooner or later, you were going to want to take off my mask. I kept envisioning you doing it when you were inside me, and wondering what your expression would be the moment you recognized me."

"Shock, that's for sure."

She wrapped her arms around herself. "Or disgust. Hatred. Humiliation. I was caught in my own trap, wanting you so badly, but terrified you still hated my guts and would regret even touching me once you knew who I was."

Chaz stopped pacing and stared down at her. "I don't hate you."

She looked up at him, her brown eyes luminous, moisture hinting at unshed tears. "I was awful to you when we were kids."

"Kids being the key word. Now that I know the adult you, I'm not about to hold childhood nonsense against you all these years later. And truthfully? I liked the attention, even if it was mostly negative! I wanted to believe my mother, that you did it because you had a crush on me."

She laughed humorlessly. "And I *didn't* want to believe mine, who said the same thing."

"Admit it—you were more scared I'd be furious that you'd tricked me about who you were."

She flushed, looking sheepish. "Well, yeah. That, too."

"Would you have gone through with it, anyway?" he asked, needing to know if she'd been as out of her mind with desire as he'd been.

She nodded easily. "Yes. I would have. If Sarah hadn't

been sitting on her car out front, I would have walked with you into your house and ripped off your clothes right there by the front door, like we discussed."

"*My* clothes. But not *your* mask."

Her cheeks pinkened. "Well, not if I could help it."

Points for honesty, he supposed.

"And then what, you were going to sneak away while my back was turned? Were you ever going to tell me?"

She hesitated. He almost saw the wheels spinning in her mind as she debated how forthright to be.

"Lulu?" he prodded, his tone promising her she'd regret it if she lied.

Finally, she admitted it. "No. At that moment, I just wanted to have you, to store up some amazing memories, and then let us go back to being friends."

He gritted his teeth, crossing his arms over his chest to control his anger. "That's pretty damned cold. As is what you've put me through for the past month."

She leapt up and stalked over. "What I've put you through? How on earth do you think it made me feel when you started sniffing around that red-haired twit, giving her credit for everything you and I had done?"

"Hopefully it made you feel like shit. Because you deserved to."

She stilled, visibly deflating as her anger left her.

"Touché."

They both fell silent for a moment, and he sensed she was as lost in thought as he. The truth had come out, everything was in the open. They'd come so far, shared so much, physically and emotionally. The question was, where did they go from here?

Was it even possible that he and Lulu could have some kind of normal relationship? Did she want to? Did he? And could he ever really trust her after she'd proved herself capable of such dishonesty and stunningly good secret-keeping?

She was the first to speak, and it was as if she'd read his mind. "Chaz, I'll understand if you can't forgive me, but please know I truly am sorry. I have suffered for being such an idiot. I've learned my lesson, and I promise you, I will never lie to you, or keep secrets from you, ever again."

He nodded slowly. "I hope you mean it. Because I really hate liars."

"I know that." She came closer, twining her fingers in the hair on his chest, licking her lips and looking up at him. "But the truth is, I don't want to lose you. I don't want to lose *this* now that we've finally discovered it."

A smile tried to tug at his lips, but he hid it. "Lose what?"

"This…connection," she admitted, gesturing toward the rumpled bed where they'd spent so many wild hours.

"You want to keep sleeping with me?"

"As long as we don't spend all our time sleeping."

More honesty. More points. He liked this adult, open and blunt Lulu Vandenberg.

"What about during the rest of our waking hours?" he asked, aware that was the bigger issue.

How on earth could the two of them develop any kind of real relationship with all the baggage and all the garbage? Awkward enough to have an affair with someone who lived two doors away—they'd never have any privacy, especially with nosy neighbors and siblings.

It was also crazy to try to maintain any kind of real relationship when he could be off for months to another country after the first of the year.

Plus, they were so different now. He was hard-nosed, always after the truth, after the story. She was dreamy, her bleeding heart worn on her sleeve these days. Passionate about her job with a group he'd heard was shady.

And they knew each other too well, had spent seventeen years living next door to each other, jealous of every shared birthday, fighting over stupid crap like Halloween costumes or holiday parties.

Oh, and then there were their siblings. Their parents. Their families. God, wouldn't this affair throw all of their relatives into a tizzy as they began taking sides, tensing up, preparing for the inevitable day when Lulu and Chaz, who had never managed to get along very well, imploded and brought both families down with them?

"Stop trying to figure everything out, at least for now," she whispered, lifting her arms and encircling his neck. She moved even closer, until her bare legs brushed his, and the peaks of those soft breasts pressing against the silk seared his chest.

"What did you have in mind?"

"We're both off work today, and it's a long weekend. We don't have to leave this apartment. We don't have to make plans or think about anything except spending the next three days exploring every erotic possibility either of us has ever fantasized about."

His resolve melted, the arguments drying up and blowing away before he'd even had a chance to verbalize them.

She was right. Outside, the world would give them grief.

In here, at least for the next three days, they could pretend that world didn't exist.

He dropped his hands to her waist and undid the bathrobe tie. "Every single fantasy, huh?"

She nodded slowly, licking her lips, staring at him through eyes glazed with desire.

"Including that one you had last night when I threatened to spank you?"

She sucked in a surprised breath, as if shocked he'd read her mind so easily. Christ, how could he not when she wore her emotions on her face? Well aware what she was imagining—picturing him spanking her, and then making it up to her as erotically as possible—had made it tough to hold onto his justified anger.

"You…you knew what I was thinking?"

"I had a pretty good idea."

She hesitated, a long, heated moment, before whispering, "Good. Then I won't have to take the time being shy about what I want. We can just get started."

10

As promised, Lulu and Chaz didn't leave her apartment for three full days. They barely left her bed for that long.

They slept a lot, talked a lot, made love a *whole* lot.

They laughed and played and indulged every erotic whim. She honestly didn't know where he got his stamina, or how he could get aroused again and again. And again.

He gave her all the credit, which she happily accepted.

Lulu wasn't a great cook, but she had enough food to sustain them, and when they ran out, they ordered in. They turned off their phones and ignored the world.

Lulu did go to the door when Marcia knocked Saturday morning. Chaz stayed in the bathroom, using a new toothbrush she'd scrounged up for him, and Lulu assured her neighbor she was fine. Making an excuse about not wanting the pregnant woman to catch whatever had made her ill at Thanksgiving dinner, she'd thanked her for her concern and then closed the door—and the world—out again. She'd returned, giggling, to Chaz, who immediately joined her, naked, in her bed.

Wrapped in their own secret world, where jobs, histories, childhood grudges, secrets, lies and families didn't exist, they lived only for the pleasure they could give to one another.

But their idyll had to come to an end, and Monday rolled around far too soon. It brought with it jobs, commutes, cold weather, the holiday season and harsh reality.

"I should really go back to my place," he told her as her alarm went off at 5:45 a.m. Monday. "I haven't shaved since Thursday morning and only have the clothes I wore over here that night."

"I like that scruffy look on you." She ran a hand over his stubbled jaw, loving how hot and sexy he looked in the morning, all raw, untamed male. She also liked how that stubble felt on her breasts, her stomach, her thighs. Yum. "And it's not as if you've been wearing your clothes, they're perfectly clean," she said with an eyebrow wag.

"You keep tearing them off me every time I try to get dressed."

"Pot, meet kettle," she said, rolling over and grabbing her shredded pajama top off the bedside table, where she'd tossed it after he'd ripped it open Thursday night. "You did some literal tearing, buddy."

His smirk was entirely male, entirely self-satisfied. "I'll buy you another one."

"Fine. Silk. Victoria's Secret. Wow me."

"That sounds like a challenge."

"Maybe it was." She got up to head to the bathroom, yelping when he swatted her bare backside as she passed him. "Haven't you left yet?"

He grinned wolfishly, trying to pull her down to the bed.

"Go! Get outta here. I can't be late, I'm too new to my job and I'm saving my few days of leave for the week before Christmas."

"Does that mean you don't want to share a shower?"

His tone was so innocent, somebody who *hadn't* showered with him might be fooled into thinking he actually meant bathing. But the last three showers they'd shared had ended up with one or the other of them pinned against the tile wall while they had hot, wet, steamy sex. They'd always run out of water long before they were finished washing.

"No. I'm finished for now. You have serviced me well," she said, tossing her head and sauntering away.

She began to walk away, but he leapt up and followed, grabbing her from behind and putting his arms around her waist. He pulled her back against him, nuzzling her neck, trying to seduce her. "Serviced you, huh? I don't know, there might be a spot left on your body I haven't tasted yet."

She quivered against him, memory assaulting her. "No. There's not. Trust me on this." Oh lordy, there most definitely was not.

He turned her around and caught her mouth in a kiss. She wrapped her arms around him, indulging in the kiss for as long as she dared, then stepped out of his arms and shoved him away.

"Now, beat it. Take that ugly yellow shirt of yours and go home." She offered in a tiny grin. "I'll meet you back here in twelve hours."

He nodded his agreement as he tried to find his clothes, which were strewn around her room. "What's the matter with my shirt?" he asked as he dug it out from under her dresser and picked it up.

"It's hideous," she said. "It makes you look like a bumblebee."

"Gosh, you're so tender and romantic after you've been shagged for four straight nights."

She stuck out her tongue at him, loving that they could go right back to being playful antagonists after being such intimate lovers. The last thing she wanted, when all was said and done, was to lose her newly found friendship with Chaz.

Of course, she didn't want to lose him as her lover, either.

Hell, she just didn't want to lose him. She wanted him in her life, in every way.

They'd pretty much agreed that was impossible, and had hidden out specifically so they wouldn't have to admit to the world what they were doing. As if they could just have a hot, secret fling that was nobody's business but their own.

Now, though, she feared it wasn't going to be that simple. Or that she'd be satisfied with just a hot, mindless fling. Amelia and Viv had pointed the truth out to her last weekend, that she wanted more than that with Chaz, she'd just been forcing herself not to think about it. Especially since he'd given absolutely no indication he wanted more. His world-traveling feet were probably already itching to get back overseas, and her job would only get more demanding as she got more involved.

Still, she couldn't change how she felt. She dreaded him leaving, dreaded going back into her regular life, pretending nothing was different.

The truth was, everything had changed.

He was a part of her now, he'd claimed her, body and soul, and she honestly didn't know how on earth she would ever return to being just Lulu, singular, and not part of Lulu and Chaz.

For all their agreements and discussions the other night…she wanted him in her life permanently. And not just as an old family acquaintance and neighbor.

She was falling in love with her friend.

Lulu let herself think it and accept it as she showered, glad he'd kissed her goodbye and left before she'd gotten in the water. She doubted she'd have been able to get out and face him without showing everything that was in her heart and in her mind. She needed some time away from him in order to try to decide how to handle this.

She could let it ride, just float along with what they were doing until they were exposed and forced to decide, for once and all, what they might mean to each other.

But that seemed risky, and a little dishonest. She'd just promised him she wouldn't lie or keep secrets. Then again, she hadn't agreed to reveal every emotion the moment she had it.

No, this was too new, too fresh and vulnerable. She had to nurture her feelings, let them develop, and then she'd figure out what to do. After all, she and Chaz had done a really good job over the past few days of starting a clandestine affair. They could keep it up for a while longer.

She was smiling about that as she let herself out of her apartment and locked the door. He was meeting her in front of his house in a few minutes so they could take their usual walk to the train station. She looked forward to walking past the regulars at the station and on the train, knowing the two of them shared a secret unsuspected by anyone else in the world.

"So, you and Chaz, huh? Figured that was coming."

Lulu almost dropped her keys as she spun around to see Peggy on the landing of the stairs, right down the hall. Dressed for work, the other woman had arrived at the perfect time to shock Lulu into utter stillness.

She tried to brazen it out and play dumb. "I beg your pardon?"

"Was it pardon you were begging for at about two o'clock Saturday morning? Because, I heard you yelling 'please' but I wasn't sure what, exactly, you were asking for."

Lulu willed the floor to open so she could sink into it, but the damned wood and carpet remained in place.

"I guess you were also praying for whatever it was you wanted, because I also heard a lot of 'Oh, God's thrown in there as well."

"I hate you."

The woman snorted with laughter. Someone else chuckled, too, and she watched as Marcia descended behind her wife, her smile just as broad, her wink knowing.

"Did you two even come up for air over the past three days?" the petite brunette asked.

Lulu buried her face in her hands. "This sucks."

"In case I haven't made it clear," said Peggy, showing no mercy, "your bedroom is sandwiched between ours above and Florence and Sherman's below. And this old house has some thin walls."

"Has everyone been discussing my sex life this weekend?" she wailed.

"Well, I don't think the neighbors in the next building have mentioned anything, do you Marc?"

Marcia tapped her finger on her cheek, as if in contemplation, and shook her head. "No, pretty sure they haven't. But the day's early yet."

Lulu's eyes narrowed. "You do know that sounds travel both ways, but I've been far too polite to mention it."

"Hey, we're married," said Peggy. "Perfectly respectable. You… Damn, girl, if good old Chaz could make you scream that way, I'm half curious about what it would be like with a dude."

Marcia frowned.

"Kidding honey," said Peggy, slipping an affectionate arm around the other woman's waist.

Finally relenting, Marcia came over and took Lulu's hand. "I'm sorry, she's such a matchmaker, and we wanted you and Chaz together. We were so happy…but we shouldn't have teased you."

"Please, don't let on to him that we had this conversation, okay?"

"Are you kidding? I want to give him a cigar or something," said Peggy.

"Oh, no, I'm begging you. He is adamant that nobody can know about this. It's just so…complicated."

Marcia nibbled her lip. "Um, Lulu, there's no way anybody who was sitting at that dinner table on Thursday didn't know."

"That's impossible."

"Well, maybe Heather. She's as dumb as a brick," said Peggy. "I don't think Chaz's hints that she should leave could have been any broader if he'd said, 'Hey, girl, I want the other one, get out.'"

That made her smile. She hadn't asked Chaz about the specifics of what had happened after she'd burst out of his house the other day. But she was glad Heather wouldn't be coming around anymore.

"The others, though, well, everybody made a pretty obvious assumption about why you skedaddled, and why Chaz got so quiet afterward. Even his jabber-jaw sister shut up and hid her giggles."

"Oh, no, Sarah figured it out? She'll tell his family, and his mom will tell my mom, and then they'll start making in-law jokes, and then when Chaz and I fall apart, they'll start trading insults and defending us. It's freaking Sarah and Lawrence all over again."

Marcia hugged her. "I wouldn't worry. I think your brother and Chaz's sister are staying busy enough to keep their noses out of your business."

That probably shocked her more than anything else. Lulu's jaw unhinged. "No way!"

"If they didn't crawl out of bed to come to Thanksgiving dinner, I'll cancel my membership in the L-club," said Peggy, snorting with laughter again.

Lulu wanted to throw her head back and groan in frustration. That was all she and Chaz needed—more Sarah and Lawrence drama to get the families drawing up battle plans again.

Then she thought about it a little more. If their younger siblings had resumed their relationship, they wouldn't be anxious for anybody to hear about it, either. Meaning they'd have to do some quid pro quo. They couldn't out Lulu and Chaz without risking their own secret.

She hoped and prayed her brother would keep Sarah's gabby mouth shut. Lawrence was very aware that his and Sarah's breakup in high school had nearly ended a whole bunch of friendships, from grandparents on down, since everybody was friends with everybody in their small town. It had practically started a war.

No, he wouldn't risk it. And he'd keep Sarah quiet.

Which meant she and Chaz should be safe for a little while. At least long enough to figure out what on earth they were doing and where they were headed.

CHAZ HAD NEVER been more tired…or more happy.

For the past two weeks, he'd been working his usual schedule, but his nights had been very active and pretty sleepless.

He just couldn't get enough of Lulu. He tried, several times, to go home and spend a normal night, alone, to regain some distance and some sanity. He'd tell himself one night off wouldn't kill him, that she had to be exhausted and getting tired of sex—women did, he'd heard.

But not Lulu. Every time she had him, she wanted him again. Just as he did her. Maybe someday the intensity would wear off and they'd be able to go a few days without touching…but he had no idea when that day might come. For right now, neither of them were anywhere close to sated or tired of their intimate games.

No matter how good his intentions, just the sight of her smiling at him from across the Metro train, or the sound of her laughter as they chatted during their walk home, would be enough to rev his engines. They'd part ways, pretending to be just commuting buddies, going into their respective buildings. Then one or the other would call, and he'd be at her place, or, more often, she'd be at his. They'd fall into bed, or on the floor, or on the kitchen table, and would lose themselves for hours in the kind of intense eroticism he'd never experienced before in his life.

He just couldn't get enough of her. When they weren't in bed, all he thought about was getting her back there.

Like right now.

"Are you sure you don't just want to go home and get naked?" he asked her.

"No," Lulu said, her tone scolding. She cast a look around to see if they'd been overheard in the store where they were shopping. "We have to get this done tonight. I don't want to come back out in *this* again."

She'd invited him out to do some Christmas shopping. He'd said yes, even though he'd rather be back in the Middle East interviewing terrorists than braving a D.C. mall ten days before Christmas.

Still, it had to be done. Plus he'd figured it would be a good chance to do something normal and nonsexual with Lulu. He loved spending time with her no matter what they did, and this seemed pretty laid-back and easy—in contrast to the rest of their relationship.

And then she'd made the mistake of walking that sexy walk right in front of him. And she'd licked that Ben &

Jerry's ice cream cone, looking damned orgasmic with every taste.

Hell, she just had to glance at him with that secretive, dark-eyed stare that said she was thinking of something she wanted him to do to her and shopping became the last thing on his mind.

"I'm Christmased out," he told her. "Why don't you just get your mother a gift card?"

"Stop whining, you big baby."

He sighed and shut his mouth, wondering how anybody could be expected to be cheerful here, in this high-end shopping mall filled with desperate-to-get-a-deal revelers.

Cheerful music erupted from every speaker, bells rang, costumed elves darted about giving away prizes and breaking into carols at the least provocation. And the decorations…good grief, it looked like Christmas had crawled in here and died.

But Lulu was smiling. Oh, that amazing Lulu smile.

She passed money to the bell ringers, stopped to listen to every jingling elf's song, had a smile and a "Merry Christmas!" for every clerk and salesperson. She loved the holidays, always had, as he recalled. While he was sick of being here, and bored to tears trying to offer an opinion on whether her mother would like the blue sweater or the gray, he couldn't deny he was enjoying watching her.

Happiness oozed from her, she radiated good cheer, and looked more beautiful than ever. He couldn't take his eyes off her, and noticed just about every man they passed reacted the same way. He wanted to stake his claim on her, but as what? Her boyfriend? Her lover? Her friend with benefits? He had to get her out of the mall and back to the only place their relationship made sense—the bedroom.

"Come on, babe, we've been here for hours. You must be wiped out." He leaned close, putting his hands on her shoulders and gently kneading. "After such a long day of work, and fighting these crowds, don't you want a nice back rub and a hot bath?"

She sighed with pleasure, dropping her head back to lean on his shoulder, and for a second, he thought he had her.

But she quickly jerked away and glared at him. "Stop tempting me! I have to finish my shopping. Lawrence and I are leaving Friday to drive out to my parents' for the holidays, and I don't want to even try to find gifts once we're there."

He understood why, knowing the finest shopping establishment in their tiny hometown was a dollar store. But her comment reminded him of something else. "Are you sure you don't want to wait until Saturday and ride out with me and Sarah?"

She glanced away, studying a cashmere scarf, avoiding his gaze. "I think it's better if we arrive separately, don't you?"

"Not really. Why wouldn't we car pool? The families might think it more strange that we didn't."

Meeting his eyes, she admitted, "I'm not sure I can sit in a car with you for four hours and not let on to Sarah and Lawrence that I'm imagining you naked or remembering what your mouth tastes like."

He swallowed hard. Her tone was utterly sincere, she was genuinely worried. But he couldn't even think that far ahead. He could only think *mouth, Lulu,* and *taste,* and then wanted nothing more than to drag her out of here. He'd maybe get her as far as the car before he had to kiss the taste right out of her mouth.

She read his mind, her face grew flushed, then she turned and grabbed a sweater—blue—and strode to the checkout counter.

After that, she shopped with less enthusiasm, and he knew she was thinking naughty thoughts. She confirmed that when she led him, casually—but with definite purpose—toward a back corner of the high-end store in which they'd ended up. Chaz followed, seeing that look in her eye—the daring look she'd worn on Halloween night. The look that said she was in the mood to do something outrageous, something dangerous. He could hardly wait to find out what.

They got to a section of the store laden with racks of nightgowns, sexy panties, bras and other undergarments and he began to get the picture.

"We're not shopping for your mother anymore, are we?"

"No, I'm all done. But I might have to buy *you* a present."

"I'll have…this," he said, gesturing toward a green silk teddy. "As long as it's the wrapping and you are the present."

She ran her fingers across the teddy, and Chaz's heart skipped a beat. When she tested the fastening of a garter belt, attached to a silky pair of hose on a mannequin's leg, he gulped down a hearty helping of want.

But then she picked up a filmy nightgown that had a front, a back, a bow connecting them on each hip, and absolutely nothing else. When she headed for the changing room, he walked after her like a panting dog.

It was late on a weeknight, near closing time. The mall had been crowded—packed, actually—with holiday shoppers earlier in the evening. But the place had thinned out a lot in the last half hour. And this lingerie area, in the back corner of a huge anchor store, was deserted, the nearest register closed, the next a whole department away.

Interesting possibilities presented themselves.

"I think I should see that on you," he said as he fol-

lowed her around a corner and into the changing area.
There was a lounge, with sofas and mirrors, where women
could come out and view their selections from all sides.
Or, he suspected, so men could view them—because the
furnishings were masculine, and a sign said men were invited to sit and wait for their companions, but shouldn't
proceed past a certain point.

He didn't sit. He proceeded.

Lulu glanced over her shoulder, spying him coming
after her, correctly reading his expression, as he correctly
read hers.

"Can you help me unzip?" she asked, so innocent, so
coy.

"I'll help you out of anything you care to take off."

She nodded, stepping into one of the private changing
booths. He walked in after her, pushing the full-length
door shut behind him. The area was as big as a decent-size
closet, with a mirrored wall and a plush bench seat. Very
upscale. Very welcoming. It was as if the store *wanted*
their customers' boyfriends and husbands to follow them
in here, as if they intended the place to be perfect for trysts
and daring escapades.

Well, that's the way he looked at it, anyway.

"Turn around," he said.

She did, waiting patiently as he unzipped her tight skirt.
He let his hands slide it down slowly, his knuckles brushing against her rear as he leaned in and smelled her hair.

Their eyes met in the mirror. She was unbuttoning her
blouse, easing each tiny, satin-covered button free of its
hole with calm, steady deliberation.

She licked her lips. Her eyes were wide and dreamy,
her breaths audible in the otherwise silent compartment.

Chaz pushed the skirt off her hips, stepping back a tiny
bit so it could drop to the carpeted floor. She finished un-

buttoning her blouse, and pushed it off her shoulders, letting it join the skirt.

"Jesus," he said, realizing she must have already done some lingerie shopping before now. He had never seen her in the stunningly sexy getup she wore.

Her black bra was lacy and was meant more to push her breasts up to dizzying, dangerous heights than to cover them. He could see a hint of her nipples peeking out the top, and he growled hungrily at the reflected sight.

But that wasn't all. He almost howled when he lowered his attention and saw the garter belt fastened around her slim waist. Four sexy, lacy seams dropped down to attach to silky stockings, but above the top hem of those stockings, she was utterly bare.

"I think you forgot something when you went to work this morning," he growled, dropping his mouth to the nape of her neck and nipping her.

"I was a good girl. I wore my panties to work."

"Did you drop them somewhere? Should we check the lost-and-found?"

She licked her lips, their stares locked in the mirror. "Maybe you should check your pocket."

Never looking away from her, he reached into the pocket of his jacket, his fingers meeting silky softness. Drawing the tiny clump of fabric out and seeing lacy black undergarments, he lifted them to his face and breathed deeply. "Yeah. They're yours."

"Was there any doubt? Was some other woman dropping underwear into your pocket?"

He dropped his mouth to the nape of her neck and kissed her, sucking lightly, realizing he'd leave a mark but not giving a damn. "No, but I'd know yours anyway. I'm addicted to your scent."

"Is that all you're addicted to?" she asked, arching her

back, tilting her bare bottom in invitation until it pressed against the front of his trousers.

He slid his hands down her sides, cupping her hips, then reaching forward to stroke her creamy stomach. Pulling her tighter against him, he watched in the mirror as her eyes flared wide and her face flushed when she felt his rock-hard erection.

God, he liked this, liked coming at her from behind, watching her reflection as he caressed her. She was unable to hide a single thought, a single reaction. She wore her pleasure on her face, and when he smoothed his hand up to cup her breast, she gasped and pushed even harder against his groin.

His hand was big and dark against her pale skin. She looked vulnerable, utterly feminine. Working the front of her bra down, he watched her nipple pop free, and caught it between his fingers. She was so responsive, he knew she felt each tweak throughout her body, knew that him playing with her nipples made her wet.

She leaned back, turning her head to gaze up at him. He bent to catch her mouth in a kiss, remaining behind her. One of her arms came up to encircle his neck, and with her other hand, she reached back for his crotch. When she struggled with his belt, he took over, undoing it, and then unfastening his pants and pushing them down, out of the way.

Lulu lifted her head and looked at his reflection in the mirror again, her face dreamy, hungry.

"Please," she whispered, putting a hand on the glass to brace herself. She made her demands even more clear, bending farther, arching toward him, inviting him to take her from behind.

He had never gotten a better invitation. Nudging her legs farther apart, groaning at the feel of those soft, silky

stockings against his skin, he reached down and parted
her cheeks. She bent over even more, until he could see
the tempting pink flesh between her legs, all slick and wet,
just waiting for him. Lulu was utterly aroused; maybe she
had been since she'd snuck away to slip her panties off and
drop them into his pocket. God knows he would have been
hard all night if he'd reached in, felt them there, and realized she was naked beneath her skirt.

"Take me," she ordered, staring into the mirror, watching him eye her lustfully.

"Yes, ma'am," he said, easing his cock into her, watching himself disappear between her welcoming folds.

Wet heat enveloped him; he sank into utter perfection,
savoring every bit of her he could take.

When he moved too slowly, she pushed back, taking
more, greedy and impatient.

Her impatience snapped the last of his control. He
gripped her hips, digging his fingers into her flesh, and
slammed into her, plunging so hard his balls slapped her
ass.

"Oh, yes!" she groaned. She quickly bit her lip, cutting
off her cries of ecstasy.

It was a little late to think about who else might be
around. He honestly didn't give a damn if anybody heard
them. It would take a gun to his head to make him stop
what he was doing.

He thrust again and again, gripping her hips and pulling her back toward him with every forward thrust. He
slammed into her with every ounce of himself and her en-
ergetic movements and satisfied sighs told him how much
she loved it.

It was insane, risky, wild. Like on Halloween night,
they were both past caring about niceties, or witnesses,
or danger. They were lost to everything but each other.

Only, this time, neither of them were playing games. There was no question of stopping, no possibility of running away.

He had her, she was his to do with what he would.

And he was hers.

11

LULA HAD FEARED things were going too well to last.

Two days later, when she and Chaz were getting on the Metro to go home, they bumped into his reporter friend, Tonia, the blonde who'd monopolized his attention at the kickball game several weeks ago. He'd told Lulu the other woman was just a colleague, which was fine. But, when pressed, he had also admitted they'd maybe been a little more to each other, at least briefly. That wasn't so fine.

Lulu hadn't even been in the picture when he and Tonia had their affair, but she was still jealous of anyone who'd ever had what she considered hers—namely, his body and his sexual attention. She'd staked her claim on Chaz, whether publicly or not. She thought of him as her own, and didn't even want to consider any of the women he'd had before she'd come back into his life. Especially not the pretty, sexy, smart ones. Like Tonia.

Maybe she was being stupid, maybe she had no right. He'd certainly never told her he loved her, never made plans, never talked about any kind of a future. But she had to believe he was thinking along those lines, as was she. She couldn't bear to imagine she'd fallen hopelessly in love with him and he didn't feel the same.

He does. This is real. It's not just the sex.

She mattered to him.

"Chaz, I'm so glad I ran into you!" the reporter said. "I never see you anymore since they moved me to the northern Virginia office."

"How are you doing, Tonia?" His smile seemed forced. Perhaps he, too, was disappointed that he and Lulu wouldn't be able to silently flirt with each other from opposite seats on the Metro train.

"I'm great. And so, obviously, are you," she said, casting an appreciative eye over him.

She was right. Chaz had always been hot, but lately he'd had that well-done look that a man wore when he was getting laid a lot. Something about that look attracted other women. It was as if they could smell sex on a satisfied man.

Lulu cleared her throat to announce her presence, wanting the female reporter to know who'd put that look on Chaz's handsome face.

Tonia turned around and glanced down at her, feigning surprise, although Lulu was sure she'd spotted her the moment she boarded the train. "And you're Lulu, right?" the woman said. "Isn't this a happy reunion?"

"Yes. Nice to see you again." Gee, that had almost sounded sincere.

"Chaz, you are just the man I wanted to meet," the woman said, swinging around and plopping down on the edge of Chaz's seat, blocking him from Lulu's view. She glanced over her shoulder. "You don't mind, Lulu, do you? It's shop talk."

Lulu shrugged, but she glared daggers at the back of the woman's head when she turned to face Chaz and drag him into quiet conversation. Lulu barely paid attention to the subject until she heard Tonia say, "I have a source who's going to give me all the dirt on that shady *Hands Across The Waters* organization."

Her jaw falling open, she looked over Tonia's head into Chaz's face. His expression was strained; he actually winced in reaction. "Tonia, I really don't think…"

"No, seriously. And I know how much you love to expose fraud and shysters. I've sensed for months that there was something going on with that place—those founders are just too squeaky clean to be true. I'm going to bring them down, and I want you to help me."

"Excuse me," Lulu said, "what, exactly, are you talking about?"

Tonia glanced over, gave her a dismissive shrug, and said, "Oh, just a story I'm doing that Chaz helped me with."

"He did, huh?"

"It was a while ago," Chaz said, his tone pointed, his expression begging her not to jump to conclusions.

She was jumping, of course. Lulu was just the jumping sort. And Tonia made jumping so very easy.

"Oh, don't sell yourself short. You're a genius at this stuff."

"Tonia and I bounced some ideas around," he explained. "I gave her some suggestions about researching the story."

Lulu bared her teeth. "Was that before or after you found out that I worked for *Hands Across The Waters?*"

His reporter friend shot up from her seat. "Oh, God, seriously?"

"Yeah. Seriously."

"I had no idea!" She gaped at Chaz. "Did I just ruin this? Is that why you're with her? Were you helping me out, trying to get an in for me?"

"He's been getting *in,* honey, but it has absolutely nothing to do with you," Lulu snapped, fury making her reckless and crude. But oh, it had been satisfying, especially when the other woman flinched. Chaz, meanwhile, looked like he couldn't decide between laughter and shock.

Tonia's mouth got smaller and tighter. "Thank you for being so…blunt. But that's really none of my business."

"Oh, sorry, I thought you were already prying into something that wasn't any of your business. Isn't that what you reporter types do?"

"That's ridiculous."

Lulu cut her off. "Well, it sounds like that's what you're doing to my employers. But let me tell you, Jenna and Felix Bernardo are the most honest, open, generous people I've ever met." She laughed, without humor. "Good luck finding dirt on them, because, frankly, it doesn't exist. You're going on a snipe hunt."

The other woman, who appeared thoroughly jaded, gave her a pitying smile. "Look, you haven't been around the world like Chaz and I have. *Nobody's* that honest, open and generous. When you're a little older, maybe you'll realize people just aren't that good and decent, not unless something's in it for them."

She could have taken a shot at the woman for the age crack, pointing out that Tonia was obviously several years older than she. But that was almost too easy. So she instead said, "Wow, you're really bitter, aren't you? I feel sorry for you if that's your take on life."

"Are you willing to talk to me about your experiences there? Maybe between us we can find out the truth. Wouldn't you like that? I could protect you as a source, keep you anonymous."

"Are you high?"

One of the woman's perfectly plucked eyebrows shot up and she stiffened, more offended than ever. "Look, I'm just doing my job."

"Well, your job sucks."

Tonia glanced at Chaz. "She doesn't have a very high opinion of *us,* does she?"

Her dismissal of Lulu was deliberate and noticeable. Chaz was stiff-jawed, and his angry expression should have sent a warning to Tonia.

She didn't notice it. "This is my stop. I'll talk to you about this later, Chaz, all right?" Her smile was a little too intimate. "Maybe we can meet up before the holiday break at that place we like so much."

She cast a triumphant glance at Lulu. If it hadn't been clear that Chaz had slept with the woman in the past, Tonia's expression would certainly have cemented the fact.

Before the other woman turned away, Chaz said, "Write your own damn story, Tonia. I am not at all interested."

Her smile faded. She flounced toward the front of the car, having to grab a security bar to avoid falling on her ass and ruining her exit. The train reached the station, and she pushed her way through the oncoming crowd to exit.

As the train filled with weekday commuters, everyone was jostled, and Lulu couldn't maintain her footing. Despite being furious, she tumbled into the empty seat beside Chaz.

"Lulu, I didn't set out to do anything behind your back."

"Oh, really? Because it sounds to me like you knew that woman was *trying* to find something bad to report about my employers, people I really respect, and you never said a word to me."

"She mentioned it," he said, "but honestly, I'd forgotten all about it. I haven't seen Tonia in a couple of weeks. I've been focusing on preparing for my next overseas assignment."

If he noticed her shock about that little nugget, he didn't let on.

"Tonia's got this obsession, but I don't share it. Between the time I've been spending with you, the series of articles from my Pakistan trip, the interest from *Time* magazine, and my research to prepare for an investigative trip to Syria after the first of the year, I just haven't thought about her since I saw her last."

Lulu had no idea where to begin. Her head was reeling.

He'd helped another reporter with an exposé on an organization that she knew was doing wonderful work? *Time* magazine? Freaking Syria? Would he again take side trips into war zones and would she be the one who didn't get the call when he was injured since he didn't want to "worry" anyone?

And he had never even mentioned any of this to her?

It suddenly hit her. She'd fallen wildly in love with someone, assuring herself he felt the same way, when the truth was they shared nothing. Absolutely nothing except sex. Amazing sex. Astounding sex. The best sex of her life, hands down.

But nothing else.

He didn't trust her with his ambitions or his dreams. He hadn't even bothered to tell her he was going into yet another danger zone after the first of the year. Come to think of it, she didn't even know where his office was, which damn stop he got off at, who he went to lunch with.

They had sex, and when they didn't have sex, they talked and thought about having sex. Oh, yeah, and they'd shopped once, finishing the shopping trip by, surprise, having amazing sex in a public place.

That was all she was to him, all their relationship was. A wild but secret sexual affair. One he could walk away from without a second glance and nobody would ever be the wiser.

She'd agreed to those terms in the beginning. Now, though, when she realized just how much of his life he'd excluded her from, she felt small and unimportant. She was fulfilling a need for him—often—but he wasn't giving her a single thought when he wasn't in bed with her or trying to get into bed with her. He'd warned her he didn't trust people, and for some reason she'd assumed she'd be different. But she wasn't. He didn't trust her or care about her any more than he had Tonia. She was just a distraction from his real love, journalism.

She had to be alone. Her chest was tight, her breaths came hard from her lungs. She was dizzy and could barely think, wanting to get off this moving train, away from this crush of people, and far away from *him*.

"Lulu, talk to me," he said, trying to take her hand.

She pulled it away and rose to her feet. Mumbling apologies to the people crowding around, she grabbed a bar and lurched away, moving toward the front of the train.

He got up to follow. She glanced back and snapped, "Don't. Just don't. I need to be away from you right now."

His eyes widened with surprise, and maybe hurt.

Jesus, how could he be surprised that she would react like this? Did he not see her as a person at all? Was she just a sperm receptacle for him?

She knew that wasn't fair. Chaz was a kind person, he always had been. She knew he'd never have set out to hurt her.

No, this hadn't been intentional. He'd just done exactly what they'd both decided to do: have a fling. Keep it secret. Not let it mean anything.

She was the one who'd broken the rules. She was the one who'd wanted something that wasn't there, who'd let herself begin to believe it wasn't the simple, sexual affair it was. She'd seen her own love reflected back from his eyes, but he'd never offered her any such thing.

She was the one hurting so badly she wanted to curl up in a ball and sob.

So she was the one who had to get away from him now,

before she broke down in tears and admitted the unthinkable: that she'd fallen in love with Chaz Browning. And that her heart was utterly broken.

"I JUST CAN'T BELIEVE she left without telling me," Chaz mumbled, speaking more to himself than to Peggy, who'd come downstairs to find out why he was knocking and knocking on Lulu's door the next evening. She'd told him Lulu was gone, having packed up and left the city while Chaz was at work.

"Why would she just go like that?"

"Sorry, Chaz, she said she wanted to beat the traffic heading out of the city tomorrow. Her brother was finished with his classes, her boss gave her an extra day off, so they packed up and left."

That all made sense, and he knew Peggy wasn't lying. But he still just couldn't comprehend it. God, had Lulu bought that nonsense Tonia had spewed on the train? Did she have the crazy idea that he had gotten close to her only for a damn story—one that wasn't even his own? How could she have believed that of him?

But there was no other explanation. Because there was no Lulu. She hadn't met him outside for their train ride this morning, hadn't answered his calls, hadn't met him on the way home from work. And hadn't answered his loud pounding on her door.

Now he knew why. She really was gone.

"What'd you do to mess it up?" Peggy asked, blunt as always.

"Honestly? I have no idea." He thrust a hand through his hair, trying to understand. "It was so stupid, a dumb argument over what somebody else said. She got the wrong idea about something, I tried to explain it, and she took off."

Peggy tsked and shook her head. "You shoulda shown

up at the door with a dozen roses and a ring last night, before she had the chance to sleep on it, build her anger and take off."

A *ring?* Chaz couldn't hide his shocked reaction to that idea. His jaw fell open and he actually laughed.

"Oh, that's funny? Gee, I think I'm beginning to understand why she left you." Peggy glared her disappointment. "Maybe I shouldn't have bothered to tell you she was gone."

He rushed to explain. "Oh, *I* don't think it's funny. I'm crazy in love with her, and I'd put a ring on her finger in a heartbeat if I weren't sure she'd laugh in my face."

"No woman laughs at a diamond ring. Get her a great big, shiny, ridiculously ostentatious diamond and she'll forgive you anything."

If only it were that easy.

"Not Lulu. She doesn't even want anybody to know we're together. What the hell would she say if I proposed marriage?" Something struck him. "Hell, I wasn't even aware *you* knew about us."

"Good grief, the two of you are so obvious, I'm sure the newspaper delivery guy is aware you're madly in love with each other. Hell, her own brother announced it at Thanksgiving dinner. You two have been in love for years."

"She's never said that. She made it pretty clear that she just wanted a fling, no commitments, nothing serious, absolutely nobody finding out."

"Boy are you stupid, Chaz Browning."

He leaned a shoulder against the wall and waited to find out why he was stupid. He had no doubt she was about to expound.

"From some things she's said, I gathered your families are tight, and your siblings mucked everything up a while back?"

"Definitely."

"And it's not easy for her to trust you, after you've made such a huge deal of your big international career and how it comes before anything else."

Chaz stiffened with shock. Had he been that much of an asshole about it? His career *had* come before everything else in the past. But did it come before Lulu? Had he given her reason to believe that it would?

The very idea made him nauseous.

"So of course she *says* she wants to be discreet, be cautious, keep it all a big secret. No point getting her heart invested if this thing between you is just sex and you're going to walk away after New Year's, right?"

"Actually, that sounds a lot like what she said," he murmured.

"But she didn't *mean* it, not deep down in her heart."

Peggy glanced up as someone came down from above. It was Marcia, who stepped out of the stairwell, eyeing them both.

"I was listening from upstairs. Peggy's right. Lulu is in love with you. Anyone can see it."

"And I'm in love with her," he admitted, acknowledging it himself for the first time. "I guess I always loved her a little bit. Now I love her a lot."

Only, he'd never told her. Never gave her any indication that he was carving out a place for her in his life. He supposed they'd both been keeping things hidden. One thing was sure: if he got her back, they were going to do a lot of talking.

When he got her back.

"I can't lose her," he said. "Not now that I've found her again."

Marcia patted his shoulder. "Then fix it."

"How? With roses and a ring, when I'm not sure which stupid thing I've done made her leave?"

Boy, wasn't that the ultimate male dilemma. He could be the poster child for how-to-screw-up-your-relationship-without-even-trying.

"She left because you let her think that a secret fling was just fine with you, too," Marcia exclaimed.

Peggy piped in. "Duh!"

"What? Wait, I'm in the doghouse because I *agreed* with her?"

"I suspect so," said Marcia. "A woman doesn't want to believe she's only good enough to be your dirty little secret. She wants to know you care enough about her to share your hopes, your dreams, your real life."

"Are you kidding? She knows me better than anyone. We talk for hours every night."

"In bed?"

He wasn't used to such bluntness about his sex life, but nodded.

"Tell me, you ever take her out to a movie? Or dinner? Hell, even a walk?"

"We went Christmas shopping at the mall the other night," he said, sounding defensive.

"And did you sneak her into a maintenance closet and shag her between Macy's and Gap?"

He didn't answer. His flushed face was all the answer the two women needed.

"Yeah. She thinks it's just sex," Marcia said, shaking her head mournfully. "That she's only good enough for you to fool around with, but not good enough to share your life."

"That's ridiculous."

Peggy gave him a pitying look. "We can tell that just by the way you stare at her when you don't think anybody will notice. Your feelings are written all over your face."

Marcia, patting his arm, added, "It's true. Lulu is the only one who hasn't figured out that you love her. She needs you to make it clear. She needs tenderness from you. Words, promises. Not just sperm."

Peggy snickered. "Ew. Sperm."

Marcia rolled her eyes and shook her head. "You're such an infant," she said, fondly scolding. "Remind me not to leave you alone with our child, ever."

"Sorry," Peggy said, growing appropriately serious.

"I have to make her understand that I love her and that I want a real future with her."

"Do you really?" asked Peggy. "Because that might mean you'll have to make some changes in your lifestyle. No woman wants to think she's less important than a job."

The very idea that Lulu would think such a thing shocked him. "She's more important than anything in my life. There's nothing I won't do to prove that to her."

"Even if it means you have to gallivant around the world a little bit less?"

He didn't even hesitate before answering. "If it's a choice between Lulu and the entire world…I choose Lulu."

Peggy patted his cheek. "I knew you were a smart one."

Thanking the women sincerely, and thinking about all the ideas they'd put in his head, he bid them a Merry Christmas and headed home. As soon as he got there, he picked up the phone and called Sarah, asking her if she could be ready to leave for home by tomorrow, and she immediately agreed. Promising to come by campus to pick her up, he told her it wouldn't be until after lunch.

He had somewhere to go in the morning, and a very special present to buy.

But first, he had to call his editor.

12

EVER SINCE SHE was a child, Lulu's mom and Mrs. Browning had co-chaired the town's Silent Night, Holy Night holiday festival. It was always held on the Friday night before Christmas, and always in the high school gym.

People would come with crafts to sell, baked goods to share. Practically everybody in the entire town would show up to bid each other a Merry Christmas before folks devoted themselves to their immediate families.

There would be carols sung and eggnog drunk, and the younger children would put on a pageant of the Christmas story. Invariably, some kid dressed up as a shepherd would get the giggles, while an angel lost her halo, and the back end of a camel would scratch his butt.

Hmm. She'd been that angel once, with the dangling halo. And she was pretty sure Chaz had been the ass-end of the camel at least once, though she didn't remember any butt scratching that year.

Being back here, with her family, in her hometown, was so much harder than she'd expected. She'd come home for the holiday season probably every other year since she'd left home, but never had she felt so surrounded by memories, so hemmed in by the ghosts of Christmas past.

Chaz was everywhere she looked. In her backyard, and in his. In the park, where they'd leaped into piles of leaves. On the playground, the baseball field. Every place she went was colored by a memory of something she'd done with him.

Including this festival.

Lulu tried to force her melancholy away, not wanting to spoil anyone else's holiday. She had to be cheerful and find some Christmas spirit as she finished putting the final touches on the manger scene. Her mother had asked her to set it up while she and Mrs. Browning did the other million-and-one tasks for tonight's pageant.

Lawrence was around somewhere, having been roped in to setting up tables or hooking up lights or something. It felt like the two of them were completely alone in the school, which had closed early today for the long Christmas break.

There were a few hours yet before people started to arrive, and Lulu ended up just sitting in a seat in the front row of the auditorium, remembering coming to see school plays in this very place. She smiled as she remembered Chaz's performance in a talent show in freshman year, with a group of his fourteen-year-old buddies. They'd done a Backstreet Boys number, complete with choreography. She remembered thinking at the time that he was cute enough to be a Backstreet Boy, after which she told him the Backstreet Boys were totally stupid and N'Sync was totally where it was at.

Yeah. She probably always had loved him. How on earth was she going to face him when he showed up in town tomorrow? Somehow, they had to get through the holiday season without dragging the family into their situation.

Although she worried about it, she also desperately wanted to see him. She knew she shouldn't have run away without an explanation. Chaz wasn't the guilty party here; he'd only done what he'd thought she wanted.

She'd realized she couldn't maintain a purely sexual relationship; her feelings were too entangled. But she also couldn't go on treating him like he'd wronged her. Because he hadn't.

"You okay down there, sis?"

She looked up and saw Lawrence standing on the stage. He'd been worried about her since she'd picked him up at school yesterday and dragged him out here, but he hadn't pried. She'd done him the same courtesy, not asking for any details about him and Sarah.

"I'm fine. Just thinking, remembering."

"Good memories?" he asked, brushing back an errant strand of hair, which always dangled in his eyes. He was a young man, but still had a sweet, earnest, boyish look. When they were kids, it had always made her want to pound him, because she'd feared the world would be cruel to tender-hearted boys like her brother. Now, she found him just about perfect, and hoped Sarah realized what she had.

"Some good, some bad. I guess I'm trying to rediscover the joy of Christmas."

"What's not to love?"

This year? "Everything."

"Aww, come on." He stepped to the edge of the stage, his youthful, angular face caught in the spotlights he'd been testing up in the booth. "How can you not love Mom burning the gravy, and Dad cutting too many bottom limbs off the tree so he has to go buy another one, and Uncle Warren drinking too much eggnog and Aunt Shelly complaining that nobody made sugar-free cookies?"

The memories brought a wistful smile to her mouth.

"You used to sneak into my room on Christmas Eve night," Lawrence said. "We would shine our flashlights out the window at Chaz and Sarah's house. They'd flash back so we'd all know we were on guard, waiting to catch a glimpse of Santa Claus."

She nodded. "And all of us would argue the next day over who had fallen asleep first."

"Remember how Dad always read us *'Twas the Night Before Christmas?* I was eleven when you had to explain to me that reindeer have hooves, not paws, and they were really *pausing* up on the roof."

"You dope," she said, actually laughing. "We had some great holidays."

"Definitely. Remember when you convinced me that Chaz would find it hilarious if I wrapped up a box of raisins and gave it to him as a present?"

"You should have quit while you were ahead. Or while I was."

"He loved the attention," Lawrence told her, serious and earnest. "Always. For as long as I can remember, you've both done everything you could to get the other to notice you, neither of you ever realizing why, even if everybody else knew."

"You truly believe we love each other?" she whispered.

"I'm certain of it. You always have, you always will, whether you end up together or not."

"Right at this moment, I'm thinking *not,*" she said, sniffing and blinking away moisture that rose to her eyes.

"It's the season of miracles. A time for precious moments that we value because we know nothing lasts forever and we should take whatever happiness we can while we can get it." He came to the edge of the stage and hopped down from it to stand right in front of her. "Christmas is the perfect occasion to do that, Lulu. To be happy, to love and to appreciate all the blessings in your life."

Tears swam in her eyes as she recognized that her kid brother had grown into a remarkable man. Deep and thoughtful, kind and so loving.

She got up and put her arms around him, hugging him tightly. "You're pretty wonderful, you know that?"

"I know somebody who thinks you are, too," he whispered back.

She pulled away and stared at him. But he was looking past her, over her shoulder. Confused, Lulu turned around and saw a man standing there.

It was Chaz.

He walked toward them in the shadowy darkness, saying nothing, his attention glued to her face. As he drew closer, she'd swear she spotted tenderness in his expression, but that might just have been wishful thinking.

"Hello, Lulu," he said.

She didn't reply, for once at a loss for words. She truly didn't know what to say to him. She'd hoped she'd have another day before having to face him, but he'd caught her off guard, caught her emotional and teary. Damn it.

"I'll see you later," Lawrence said, walking by Chaz and fist-bumping him.

And then they were alone.

"Merry Christmas."

She sniffed, finding a stray thought and throwing it out. "Silly, Christmas is a week away."

"For me, Christmas always started with the Friday night pageant."

Yeah, it had for her, too.

He came closer, and then closer still, until she could feel the warmth of his body radiating toward her.

"You left," he said, his expression betraying his hurt.

"I know. I'm sorry, I was being a coward."

"Why did you go?"

She blinked to keep any tears from falling. "I was dumb, blaming you for something that was never your fault."

"Oh, there was a lot that was my fault. Let's start with

the article—you don't have to worry. I talked to Tonia and got the whole story, as I should have done from the beginning. Her 'source' was a disgruntled former employee. She can't find a single thing on your employers—they're very good people. There will be no article."

"Oh, thank you," she said, relief lifting her spirits, even though she was still numb about his presence here.

He lifted a hand and cupped her cheek, brushing his thumb across her lips, searching for something in her eyes. Lulu stared back at him, wondering how things could have gone so crazy, how having a wild affair could have led her to acknowledge a truth she'd run from her entire life.

She loved this man. She wanted him for her very own, for as long as she could have him.

When his tender smile widened, she got the feeling he'd found whatever it as he'd been searching for in her face.

"Next, I don't want to have a secret affair with you anymore," he told her.

Lulu flinched, feeling like he'd slapped her. Whatever she'd expected him to say, it wasn't that.

She swallowed, hard, trying to remain calm. Not that Chaz didn't have the right to dump her—she'd acted like a jealous fishwife, when the only title he'd ever offered her was bedmate. Still, a part of her had hoped it wouldn't be that easy for him to give her up. And her heart, which she'd hoped had begun to mend, split apart all over again.

Damn it, loving this man was painful. Especially now that he had come to end things once and for all.

"All right, I understand," she said, wrapping her arms around her waist, suddenly feeling cold. "It's for the best."

"No, you don't understand," he said, brushing his fingers through a strand of her hair, stroking it tenderly. "I don't want to have a secret affair with you, Lulu, because I love you too much to keep hiding it."

She couldn't have heard him correctly. "What did you say?"

He cupped her face in both his hands, tilting her face up to his. "I said I love you," he whispered. "I always have, even when I swore to everyone who would listen that I hated you. I can't imagine myself ever being with anyone except you. You are *all* I want."

"But…but…the families! Your job, the sneaking around…"

"All second to you. I was so intent on finding the truth in dusty, far-off places, but then something Peggy said made me think about what I really want from my life. And it's not travel or a job or a magazine cover."

"What is it?" she asked, almost too afraid to hope she knew the answer.

He brushed his lips across hers, gently, almost reverently, and whispered, "It's you, Lulu. I think, deep down, it's always been you. You're everything I want, and wherever you are will be home to me. I don't need the whole world as long as I can always have one little piece of it where you are."

She trembled, hearing the certainty in his voice.

"So I phoned my boss and told him I plan on working stateside for a while. Do you think you can stand to have me around a lot of the time?"

"I can definitely stand it," she said, relief filling her. Whether they were together or not, she hated the thought of him ever being anywhere that could endanger his life. He was much too precious, too special, for the world to lose. Someday, she knew, he'd want to go to some far-off place and do his adventuring, but she'd make sure he always knew he had a place to come home to, where he was loved more than life itself.

"I'm glad you're sticking around."

"Just glad?"

"Very glad," she said, her tone and expression solemn.

"I love you," he repeated, brushing his lips against hers, kissing her with such tenderness, she almost melted on the spot. "I won't deny I want to keep sneaking around with you, just for fun. But if we do, we'll have to be pretending we're not wildly in love and that it's all just about sex."

"It's not all about sex?"

"Oh, God, no," he swore, emotion shining in his eyes. "I want you, without a doubt, and you will always drive me absolutely crazy with lust."

That didn't sound so bad.

"But I want *all* of you, not just your body. I want to hear what you're thinking and planning and dreaming. I want you to feel you can tell me anything, and that I can do the same with you."

"You can."

"I know. Because I trust you wouldn't ever betray me."

She believed him. They finally were being completely honest with each other now. Except for one thing. She licked her lips. "You're pretty sure I'm in love with you, huh?"

"Pretty damn sure, Lucille."

"Now you've gone and ruined the moment," she said with a mock sigh.

"Let me make it better." He stepped back. "I want to give you your Christmas present early."

Not sure what to expect, she had to grab the edge of the stage to steady herself when he dropped to one knee in front of her and pulled a small box out of his pocket.

"Think you could sneak around, be a secret lover and have wild, public sex with a guy you're married to?"

"What?"

"Will you marry me, Lulu?"

The world trembled, or else she did, as he flipped open the lid of the box. Inside was a ring, a sapphire surrounded by small diamonds, set in a delicate filigree. It was simple, and beautiful and absolutely perfect.

"I was told I should get you a big, shiny, obnoxious rock," he murmured, watching her closely to gauge her reaction. "But somehow this seemed to suit you better. It's honest, and lovely, just like you."

She nodded, tears filling her eyes. "Yes," she whispered.

"Yes, you like the ring?"

"No. Well, wait, yes, that, too," she said, the tears running now and her thoughts scattering in a thousand directions. "But mainly, yes, Chaz, yes, I love you. Yes, I'll marry you. Yes, I'll be your secret lover and your public wife."

She offered him her hand, noticing it tremble as he slid the ring onto her finger. It was a perfect fit. More, as he'd said, it was honest, and lovely, and had come straight from his heart. And she adored it.

"I love you, I do," she said, not waiting for him to get up, but dropping to her knees in front of him. "I've loved you long before I knew I did."

"I'm not sure you loved me the day you took the ladder away and made me break my tailbone," he said, a laugh rumbling in his chest.

"I did, too," she insisted, "I was just mad because you'd shared your Capri Sun with somebody else in the playground that day."

He gaped at her, and she blushed.

"What can I say? I'm jealous and I keep what's mine," she said. "Can you handle that?"

He nodded slowly. "I can handle that. And I promise, I will never again share my Capri Sun with another girl." He held her hands, pulling her closer. "Unless she has brown curls and dark brown eyes, just like her mother."

That was a long way off, but the idea of someday having a family with Chaz made her feel light enough to fly up off the floor.

He kept her grounded, though, pulling her close. Crushing her in his embrace, he kissed her with such love, such tenderness, she started to cry all over again, but then to laugh, as well. Emotions surged and filled her, memories washed over her, anticipation of a bright and joyous future swelled within her.

She hadn't been aware she was capable of feeling so much at the same time, and had never dreamed that the boy next door would be the one she'd trust with her heart for all the days of her life.

When the kiss ended, he lifted his head, stroked her cheek and whispered, "Should we go and tell our mothers they're going to be in-laws?"

She nodded happily, picturing it, knowing that she and Chaz had a bond strong enough that it would never break. Their families would be ecstatic, and every one of them would say, *I told you so,* and Lulu wouldn't care one bit, because she was loved and she was *in* love and it was Christmas and life was perfect.

"Yes, let's," she replied.

"Merry Christmas, Lulu, my love," he whispered as he rose to his feet, helping her to hers

She stood before him, staring into soulful eyes that shone with emotion, and replied, "Merry Christmas, Chaz Browning."

* * * * *

Don't miss the story of how Lulu's friend Amelia finds her own holiday magic in the anthology
NEW YEAR'S RESOLUTION: ROMANCE,
available January 2015!

REQUEST YOUR FREE BOOKS!
2 FREE NOVELS PLUS 2 FREE GIFTS!

HARLEQUIN®

Blaze®

red-hot reads!

SPECIAL EXCERPT FROM

H HARLEQUIN®

Blaze®

New York Times bestselling author
Vicki Lewis Thompson is back with another
irresistible story from her bestselling
miniseries *Sons of Chance!*

A Last Chance Christmas

She stood on tiptoe, wound her arms around his neck and
gave it all she had. So did he, and oh, my goodness. A
harmonica player knew what it was all about. She'd never
kissed one before, but she hoped to be doing a lot more of
this with Ben.

Although she'd never thought of a kiss as being creative,
this one was. He caressed her lips so well and so thoroughly
that she forgot the cold and the late hour. She forgot they
were standing in a cavernous tractor barn surrounded by
heavy equipment.

She even forgot that she wasn't in the habit of kissing
men she'd known for mere hours. Come to think of it, she'd
never done that. But everything about this kiss, from his
dessert-flavored taste to his talented tongue, felt perfect.

As far as she was concerned, the kiss could go on forever.
Well, maybe not. The longer they kissed, the heavier they

HBEXP79827

breathed. His hot mouth was making her light-headed in more ways than one.

That was her excuse for dropping her phone on the concrete floor. It hit with a sickening crack, but in her current aroused state, she didn't really care.

Ben pulled back, though, and gulped for air. "I think that was your phone."

"I think so, too." She dragged in a couple of quick breaths. "Kiss me some more."

With a soft groan, he lowered his head and settled his mouth over hers. This time he took the kiss deeper and invested it with a meaning she understood quite well. Intellectually she was shocked, but physically she was completely on board.

This time when he eased away from her, she was trembling. Like a swimmer breaking the surface, she gasped. Then she clutched his head and urged him back down. She wanted him to kiss her until her conscience stopped yelling at her that it was too soon to feel like this about him. "More."

**Pick up A LAST CHANCE CHRISTMAS
by Vicki Lewis Thompson,
on sale December 2014,
wherever Harlequin® Blaze® books are sold.**